Outlaws

Outlaws

Allen Cody

 SeaStory Press

Outlaws

© 2019 by Allen Cody

Illustrations by Allen Cody

Cover design by Cody Taube

Printed in the United States of America
ISBN 978-1-936818-51-8
Library of Congress Control Number: 2019908177

SeaStory Press
1508 Seminary St. #2
Key West. Florida 33040
www.seastorypress.com

DEDICATION

To my mom, who taught me arithmetic
and how to write.

To my son, Cody.

And to my editor and publisher, Sheri,
who turned this into a beautiful book.

Visual Fiction

Publisher's Note

VISUAL FICTION: A unique genre describing these short stories by award-winning screenwriter, Allen Cody. **OUTLAWS** is a collection of mythic tales transporting the reader from the depths of the sea to the stark western deserts, introducing pirates and warrior chiefs and modern-day fugitives. Allen's vivid style succinctly pictures each scene, like set descriptions in a movie script. You feel a sense of immediacy and clarity, even as the subject approaches the magical. See these narratives, and embark on unexpected adventures.

Sheri Lohr, SeaStory Press

Contents

Walk On Clouds   1

Under The Mango Tree   3

American Indian Uprising   17

    American Indian Uprising, Part Two   25

The Tree   39

Tugboat Thrasher   43

    Thrasher, Part Two—If a Tree Can Talk   57

The Healer—Shepherd Girl   79

    The Healer, Part Two   87

    The Healer, Part Three   99

    The Healer, Part Four   109

Two Caves   115

    Two Caves, Part Two   119

High Seas   123

    High Seas, Part Two   157

Pink Pearl Hunter   165

    Pink Pearl Hunter, Part Two   179

Lucky   187

Passage to Montedenero   193

Outlaw   199

Walk On Clouds

When you walk on clouds
Sometimes you fall through
But it is worth every fall
Just to have been up there.

Under The Mango Tree

GULF STREAM—FLORIDA STRAITS—NIGHT

Clouds skid across the moon and stars. Dark ocean. Dark as blood. Waves crash. Sweet Spanish guitar music plays.

A rickety Cuban refugee boat hangs sideways on top of a cresting wave for an impossible moment—and capsizes—six, eight, twelve people, women, men, children, screaming, gasping, drowning under a cold moon.

Carlita Sanchez (sixteen), a beautiful Cuban flower, sees her little brother, Juan (four) sink. "No Juanito!"

She dives under, pulls him up, he clings to her back. Carlita holds onto a piece of wood from the wrecked boat, floating, rising on each dark wave.

Clouds blow away. Stars so beautiful. Carlita whispers softly to her little brother, "...the stars are eyes of the Angels."

Carlita treads water. The Big Dipper, the golden North

Star, Polaris, low above their heads. Carlita swims. Slowly at first. To the beat of Juan's little scared heart. His tiny fingers spread beneath her throat.

Then she swims wildly. With all the life, with all the blood that pumps through both their veins.

Swimming strong and steady, on and on, toward the North Star. Toward America. Bathed in starlight. Moonlight pulsing over them like a warm silver heart.

SMATHERS BEACH, KEY WEST—NIGHT

Hidden in shadow, Carlita rocks back and forth in the sand, shaking, hugging her little brother.

Carlita: "It is just you and me now little brother. Mommy and Daddy are up there in the stars, in heaven."

KEY WEST STREET—SUNRISE—10 YEARS LATER

A rooster crows, screaming his scrawny gizzard out on the overgrown lawn of a small run-down house.

Inside, Juan, now 14, climbs into a T-shirt, heads toward the screen door. Juan has grown, a tall, clean, honor student, athletic, good-looking, strong; the kind of boy you'd want for a son.

Carlita: "Don't forget your algebra book." He opens the screen door with a creak, twists round as Carlita hands him the book and grabs him by the arm. "Wait." She kisses his cheek trying hard to hold onto the moment. "Have a great day. Do your best."

Angry, he flashes his report card, "Straight A, Sis. Come on, what, don't you think I'm doing my best? Gimme a break. Gonna be home late. Got to unload lobster traps after school."

The screen door creaks and slams shut. He's gone. Carlita realizes she blew it; stands alone, lingering regret and guilt turn sour in her mouth, he's gone. Long morning shadows fill the porch where Juan just stood. "Okay. Hey, I'm sorry, I know you do your best, I didn't mean..."

Too late, he's gone, she realizes the only thing she meant to say and didn't was, "*I love you...*"

Juan rides his bicycle.

Juan in class, sits at a desk, takes notes.

Carlita rides her bicycle through Key West streets.

Carlita waits on tables in a seedy waterfront restaurant, Conch Shell Raw Bar.

KEY WEST HIGH SCHOOL—LATE AFTERNOON

Juan unlocks his bicycle. Kids leave school, drive daddy-bought new Hummers, Jags and BMWs all around him.

He climbs on his bike and rides off.

LOBSTER DOCKS, STOCK ISLAND—SUNSET

Funky commercial lobster boats tied to a crumbling cement seawall. Wooden lobster traps stacked up in rows under open-air tin roofs.

Outlaws

Juan rests his bike on its kick-stand behind *Sandra Ann*, a rust-streaked 40-foot open boat loaded with lobster traps all marked with red floats, (each lobster boat has a different color float attached to their lobster traps).

He takes off his backpack, the high school algebra book sticks out, and lays it down beside his bike. No one else around.

A pelican watches from the end of the dock. Juan lifts a heavy lobster trap off *Sandra Ann*, carries it along the seawall and places it on a stack of traps, with coiled black lines and red Styrofoam floats attached.

Juan lifts another trap from *Sandra Ann*, carries it over to the stack and goes back for another. He pulls off his T-shirt and tosses it on the handlebars of his bike. Another lobster trap; his tight skin shines with honest sweat.

He picks up another and carries it, but it snags the corner of a trap on a different boat's stack. The trap falls to the ground, a green and yellow float attached. The pelican flies away.

Juan puts his trap down and bends over to pick up the one that fell; it's smashed. He's on his knees.

He lowers his head to see the damage in the fading light. The cement in the bottom of the trap is cracked; white powder spills out from a big torn plastic baggie, now half-imbedded in the broken cement.

A pair of feet in blue sandals beside him, the right big toe missing. Juan turns to see who it is...

A lobster trap crashes down on his head and presses him into the ground. Into the broken trap. Two big hands push the lobster trap down harder. Juan gasps for breath, white powder in his mouth and nose.

He convulses...

MOMENTS LATER—SPLASH.

Juan Sanchez' lifeless body sinks slowly into the dark, murky water. A hose washes away the white powder, and a hand and arm carries the broken lobster trap away.

CARLITA'S HOUSE—NIGHT

Phone rings. Rings again. Rings again.

SEEN THROUGH SCREEN DOOR

Carlita picks up the phone, "Yes, I am Carlita Sanchez. Yes, he is my brother. What's this about?" Carlita puts her hand over her mouth. Tears in her eyes. She collapses to her knees. "How? Drug overdose? Cocaine? Impossible."

LOBSTER DOCKS—NIGHT

Carlita stands in the dark where Juan was killed. She flashlights dried blood on the cement and kneels for a closer look.

OCEAN—NIGHT—ONE MONTH LATER

A Panamanian tanker—big, ominous, rusty—rumbles along under the stars.

STRAITS OF FLORIDA—OFF KEY WEST—NIGHT

Three wooden shrimp boats, outriggers extended, steam eastbound, rolling on a southwest swell. Onshore—the twinkling lights of Key West a mile away.

CONCH SHELL RAW BAR, KEY WEST—NIGHT

Closing time 10:30—a long slow night.

Carlita, waitress, gets ready to leave the empty restaurant.

At a table she rubs her feet, slides them into her sandals, and pulls out her tips. She stands, counts dollar bills, heads for the Ladies Room.

Inside, another waitress, tall blonde Suzi, wears a *Fast Fortune* Casino Boat T-Shirt, she leans over the sink and snorts a line of coke off a compact mirror. Suzi presses a finger to her powdered nostril, sniffs in, sees Carlita, "Hey, want some yummy blow?"

Carlita sees what Suzi's doing, spins around, slams the door. She brushes her long, shiny, black hair, as she walks through the empty restaurant. She flicks her hair to one side, opens the front door. She inhales the clean night.

Travis (28), boatbum bartender, backwards baseball cap, earring, eyes vibrate with electricity at being so close to Carlita—follows her out.

BOARDWALK—NIGHT

"Hey, Carlita, I heard about your brother."

"Yeah, well." She turns away, hiding her pain.

"I'm really sorry. Tell me if there's anything I can do. Anything."

"I… I don't understand. He was an honor student, he was so smart, he was an athlete. He never would do drugs." She wipes a tear.

"Hey Carlita, you really need to get out, have some fun, what you doin' this weekend?"

"Sleeping."

He walks beside her, pictures Carlita asleep, "Wanna go diving?"

"Mmm... well... maybe."

"Get some lobsters?"

"Maybe."

"Call you tomorrow."

"Not before noon you don't."

"Don't worry, I'm gonna sleep in tomorrow too. I gotta work tonight. Midnight to four."

"Where d'you work?"

A flash of lightning crackles above the boardwalk as they head for the parking lot.

"*Fast Fortune,* Casino Boat. First day. New deckhand."

"How could you work for those gangster slimeballs?"

"Money's good."

"You're such a slut."

"You're absolutely right. Call you noon tomorrow."

"Whatever." Carlita unlocks her bicycle.

"Want a ride home?" She points to her bike and smiles. She wraps the lock under the seat and snaps it shut.

"Sure? I can put it in back of my pickup."

"I'm sure."

"It's gonna rain."

"I love rain, won't have to take a shower before I go to sleep."

Travis closes his eyes for a second trying to imagine Carlita in the shower. He opens his eyes, "Call you at noon. Let's go diving."

"Don't hold your breath."

"Okay. See you tomorrow... I hope."

She gets on her bike, "Hey, thanks again for letting me tie my Boston Whaler behind your sailboat."

Travis climbs into his pickup truck,

"Oh, didn't I tell you? There's a tie-up fee."

"Tie-up fee?"

"You have to be my dive buddy." Travis fires up the redneck, primer-gray pickup, and revs it up. He drives off the lot—loud, thumping rap music pumps out his open window.

He pulls up to the stop sign and watches her in his vibrating rear view mirror. His fingers steady the frame so he can get a last look at Carlita. He waves, looks at her one more time, pops the clutch, burning rubber onto Caroline Street.

STREETS—BICYCLE MOVING—NIGHT

She rides. Her long hair billows in the wind. Her shirt presses against her body. Does she know how beautiful she is? It rains. Carlita moves fast down the wet narrow road.

A stretch-Cadillac comes from behind with FAST FORTUNE—CASINO BOAT magnetic signs on both doors and trunk. It splashes Carlita from head to Birkenstock.

She yells, "Jerk!" She's soaked. Now the rude stretch-limo turns right, without signaling and cuts her off. She jumps off just as the limo runs over her bike, crushing it, and drives away.

Carlita picks up her broken bicycle as if it were an injured bird. She carries it down the street, the crumby end of a long, crumby day "You're gonna pay for this!"

CARLITA'S HOUSE—NIGHT

She walks up the stairs to the porch of her little conch house, lays down her bike by the side door and pulls letters out of the mail box. Purring, her cat Angel comes to greet her. Her tail in the air, Angel rubs around Carlita's ankle.

Carlita picks her up, opens an envelope, and reads by the

light of the naked porch light bulb. She strokes her cat on the head. "Hi, Angel baby," She kisses her cat, "Looks like we have to move, again. Oh, and guess who bought the house and the whole darn block? Bicycle murderers, FAST FORTUNE INC."

Carlita puts Angel down, opens the door and walks in behind her cat, "Why can't they for once do something good with all that money?" She looks through her mail.

The inside of her house is small—nice place if you're a termite.

CARLITA'S BEDROOM

A mini welding set on a table made of saw horses and sheets of steel. Various brightly painted cut-out steel sea animals float on the walls.

A dive bag, two dive tanks, scuba gear in the corner. A black wetsuit on a hanger. Carlita screws the first stage onto a scuba tank and checks the pressure gauge... 3000 psi—full.

Carlita picks up Angel and looks into her eyes, "What's wrong, Angel?" Angel looks right back at Carlita, tilts her head sideways like she's trying to figure out what Carlita's talking about, "You just don't care any more; you used to care; now you just endure; content to just survive the day." Angel looks away, doesn't want to hear this... "Is that what happens to us?... After a while we just don't care any more? Surviving the day replaces the dream? Well damn it! I care! And it's just not fair."

Angel looks at Carlita and turns her head sideways. Carlita kicks off her sandals.

She's down on the floor doing push-ups, straining, breath blasting... 48... 49... 50 ... She sees the sandals she wore that night at the lobster docks, something is stuck to the sole—a hunk of gum stuck to a matchbook with dried blood on it. She pulls off the matchbook, printed on the cover: FAST FORTUNE INC.

She thinks about that night on the lobster docks, the flashlight, the blood, cocaine, Suzi snorting cocaine in the bathroom, the stretch limo, her mangled bicycle, Juan's broken body.

She looks at a photo of Juan in front of the net at the hockey roller rink. He wears an athlete's confidence, a black Reef Chiefs hockey T-shirt, hockey goalie pads, roller blades and a goalie stick.

She flicks off the lights, and lights the entire matchbook, holding it till it burns up. As if an oath she whispers, "*Fast Fortune,* I know what you did."

She throws the ash in the garbage can and peels off her wet clothes, pulling Juan's black hockey T-Shirt over her naked skin and plops onto bed and under the sheets.

Carlita closes her eyes. A tear for Juan. Her body wracks with sorrow, she cries herself to sleep.

Carlita asleep... She sits up, her eyes open, but she's asleep.

Outlaws

She climbs out of bed, walks into the wall, **slam!**, turns around, walks back to her bed, lies down and gets under the covers without waking up.

She sits up in bed again. Wide awake, her lips whisper, "I'm done crying for you little brother. I'm going after them for what they did to you!"

American Indian Uprising

NEW MEXICO

On a wooden stake, a post-it note flutters in the light desert breeze with the words: 1862 Chiricahau Apache Massacre Site.

A team of four archaeology students dig up remains.

One archaeologist, wearing a white lab, coat dusts off and catalogs human American Indian bones as if they were miscellaneous shards of pottery and places them in boxes labeled U of NM.

A skull of an American Indian child is casually placed in a box containing a child's small rib cage, arm and leg bones.

Scattered amongst them are Indian artifactae—arrowheads, jewelry, beadwork.

Outlaws

All are catalogued, tagged, and placed in boxes.

The vast whispering desert ripples in remorseless heat, its citizens move slowly: bee, red ant, scorpion, lizard, rattlesnake, crow—over a distant mirage an eagle carves the infinite sky.

⌣

U OF NM ARCHAEOLOGY BUILDING

Lit-up cement Archaeology Building.

Through the door, down the hall, down the stairs to the dank basement.

Moths flicker about florescent lights illuminating row upon row of boxes identical to those at the battle site—hundreds and hundreds of skulls and bones of real Indian Dead.

Some crates' lids lay pried open, revealing Indian remains.

A spider climbs out an eye socket.

NEW MEXICO—DESERT PLAIN

Windswept desert stretches before us.

A funky Navajo reservation truck rattles along the empty two-lane.

We see the rusted frame of a truck, the smoking motor jutting out in front, no hood, no fenders, no doors, no pickup bed. Just a truck frame with engine, steering wheel, two seats, part of a dashboard tied on with bungee cord, gas tank and four bald tires.

RonJon, rider, eighteen, pudgy, longhair, wearing a "Blow Me" t-shirt. And driving, Andy Smallarrow, just-turned-eighteen-skinny-acne-face-longhair-kiss-my-pimply-ass-attitude. Drinking cans of cheap beer and tossing the empties into the wind.

Andy stands up steering with his knees and yells, "FUCK THE WHOLE WORLD! FUCK EVERYONE AND EVERYTHING!"

A lone figure by the side of the two-lane watches. He is a weathered and wrinkled old Indian man, who stands in a field of creosote bush, sage and Joshua trees.

He is humble, yet noble, honest and proud.

He wears a dusty, tattered, authentic traditional outfit.

His dark leathery skin is accented with sparse but tasteful turquoise on silver jewelry.

His hair is long and graying and lifts lightly in the dry wind.

His face and hands are a deep-etched road-map of a long and hard-fought life.

He looks directly at us with wise reptilian eyes, points to Andy and RonJon and says:

"This here is the New Generation. The last hope of the Indian People."

Drinking beer and smoking, Andy tosses another empty

can out. He yells, "Another dead Indian."

RonJon slightly annoyed at Andy: "Ever hear the word recycle?"

Andy: "Fuck the fucking environment." He burps loudly, "What's the fucking environment ever done for me?"

Andy and RonJon rattle along.

Andy smacks on the truck radio.

Andy turns the dial to loud rap music.

Andy and RonJon move their heads and hands gangsta style as the loud rap music pounds from the truck which groans past in a cloud of blue smoke.

A skunk waddles across the highway.

Andy swerves to hit the animal.

The skunk raises his tail straight up into the air, stands tall and scoots the rest of the way across the road, avoiding Andy's truck's rubber.

Andy says, "I fucking hate fucking animals."

Andy and RonJon's truck clatters up to the gas pump.

Andy buys some gas, a six pack of Bud Lite and a box of smokes.

He asks the Indian gas station attendant, wearing greasy overalls, something; the attendant points thatta way.

Andy mounts the truck and they both light cigarettes, crack open cans of beer and are back on the road.

Up the road a piece, their truck hiccups to a stop.

RonJon asks, "How much gas d'you put in?"

Andy: "Two bucks."

RonJon: "Dude, gas is like three and a half a gallon, you din't even put in a gallon."

Andy: "Yeah okay, okay, but I got us some smokes and beer. Maybe we can find us some more gas-o-leene"

RonJon: "Yeah. Right, how we gonna *find* gas?"

They get out and hike up a hill to think about their situation.

On the other side, a team of three student archaeologists work a roped and staked-off site, sifting through the desert sand.

Sam, a preppy, know-it-all grad student, uses shiny archaeological dusting tools, wears new pigskin leather gloves with the fingertips clipped off.

RonJon: "Whoa, check it out."

Andy: "Grave robbers."

RonJon: "Yeah dude, grave robbers."

Andy: "Check out—in the black pickup."

In the bed is a complete skeleton.

RonJon: "Whoa dude. That could be my Uncle George."

Andy grabs an empty plastic gas can and a clear hose from his truck, "Looks like we found us some petro-le-um."

Outlaws

They sneak down to the black pickup.

Hiding behind the truck, RonJon siphons gas into the can.

Andy busy rattling around with the skeleton. Drags it out of the bed. Opens the truck's door. Sits the skeleton in the driver's seat. Wedges the skeleton's foot over the gas pedal. Puts a rock on it. Grips the skeleton's hands onto the steering wheel.

RonJon, with a full can of gas, "Okay dude, done."

Andy grabs the can from RonJon and sloshes gas on the skeleton, "Go top it off again."

RonJon tops it off.

Andy chuckles, "Hey, check this out dude."

He turns the key, lights off the skeleton and pops it into drive.

The pickup screeches off.

Andy and RonJon haul the full gas can back to their truck, laughing.

The archaeology grad students look up in horror and see their truck driving with a burning Indian skeleton in the driver's seat...

American Indian Uprising
Part Two

UP IN THE SKY—THUNDER CLOUDS, LIGHTNING

Two great War Chiefs ride up to the edge of a cloud on magnificently painted and feathered war ponies.

They are framed by patches of intense blue sky.

Meet Chief Crazy Horse on the left, and Chief Sitting Bull on the big pinto.

From the edge of the clouds they peer down at the burning truck.

At the smoldering skeleton driver.

At Andy Smallarrow and at RonJon filling up their truck with stolen gas.

And at archaeology students digging up American Indian bones at massacre sites and sacred burial grounds.

Outlaws

The Chiefs' horses snort and shake their heads.

Chief Crazy Horse and Chief Sitting Bull look farther into the distance.

Gliding past Coyote Butte and Council Pillars, past the Devil's Garden and Double Arches.

Past silver sage, desert broom, brittle bush, barrel cactus, creosote bush, cow's tongue, Apache pine and velvet mesquite.

Past Wind Cave deep in Paha Sapa, the sacred Black Hills.

Past petrified petroglyphs.

To Indian bones in boxes at archaeology buildings at universities.

At museums' Native American bones collections. The Smithsonian.

At a New England Button factory storeroom of American Indian bones.

And then through the stone walls, drunken preppy Ivy Leaguer Skull and Bone fraternity boys sneer and point at the Skull of Geronimo wearing a party hat in the glass case.

Then the frat boys pull out the savage Skull of Geronimo and toss it to each other, giggling sophomorically, like silly little girls.

UP IN THE CLOUD

Chief Sitting Bull reaches up, grabs a fat thunderbolt

mid-air.

In a loud and angry voice he bellows, "ENOUGH!"

Crazy Horse: "What you got in mind?"

Sitting Bull: "Rise up my dead Indian brothers! Rise up! You have four days until the full moon to reclaim the stolen bones of our Dead and return them to their rightful graves!"

He heaves the massive thunder bolt.

It separates into dozens of jagged lightning bolts that take off in different directions.

MASSACRE GRAVE MOUND

A lightning bolt suddenly **smashes** into the ground making us nearly **jump** out of our seats.

The earth **rattles**. Strange smoke and steam escapes from earthen cracks.

ANOTHER MASSACRE GRAVE SITE

A second lightning bolt **spears** down, scaring us half to death again—impaling the ground.

The earth **shakes**.

Lumps of earth rise and fall, moving like waves in a stormy sea.

MOUNTAIN

BAM! We jump as another noisy lightning bolt **pierces** the top of the mountain.

Outlaws

The air is ominously silent and fetid with sulfurous gas and putrid odor.

A skeletal finger **punches** through the earth.

As it feeds on air, skin and fingernails germinate on time-whitened bone.

It rises into a hard-clenched skeletal fist.

The fist opens and feels the earth around it.

It grasps a tree root and wrenches out a gnarled arm bone.

Nearby a lightning bolt **crackles.**

An Indian skull pokes through lumps of earth.

It jerks from side to side peering around through dirt-packed eye sockets.

The dirt falls away to red eyeballs, bloody patchy skin and hanks of scraggly hair regenerating on the life-giving oxygen.

With a creaking heave, the Skeletal Dead Indian **claws** his way to the surface, spitting dirt and **gasping** for sinewy strands of life and air.

Wearing rags that once were fine traditional clothing.

Wearing a war bonnet of tattered Eagle feathers.

He reaches his arms to the sun. **He is alive again!**

One at a time they rise.

More and more and more Indian Dead rising, creaking, bursting from the steaming stinking earth.

As certain as there once were dark shaggy Buffalo roaming the open plain, **THE INDIAN DEAD HAVE RISEN!**

TWO LANE ROAD

Andy's truck is parked half on the road.

Andy and RonJon stand beside it both taking a leak.

Andy raises his arms to the sky, "Aww, yes! The world is my toilet!"

They climb back in and the funky punk truck turns off and winds along the dirt road kicking up a great cloud of dust.

Andy and RonJon bounce inside, coughing and smoking a joint.

They come upon a dented Airstream Trailer, a dusty sky-blue, '50s style, rounded aluminum trailer, painted sparsely with mystical Indian petroglyph symbols.

Andy, "Wow! Grampa's at last."

They each take another hit.

Andy: "Yeah. He's got a birthday present for me. Wonder what it could be?"

RonJon: "Your grampa's kinda strange, yeah?"

Andy: "Oh yeah."

They park and finish the joint.

Andy: "He don't like if you just park and come right up and knock on his door right away."

They each take another toke.

RonJon: "Why not?"

Andy takes another: "Says travelers carry ghosts. Better for us to wait here and finish this b'fore we go up there. So's we're not travelers fresh off the road and aren't bringing no ghosts in."

RonJon: "You believe that?"

Andy: "Course not. D'you?"

RonJon: "Dunno."

A short while later, Andy's hand reaches out to knock on the door of the ancient trailer and stops. Both of them a little paranoid. They look around the parched yard—a wheel-less '40s Ford pickup sags on cinder-blocks. Their underwear sticks out about five inches above their pants.

Andy knocks on the door.

A familiar voice comes through the door—Grandfather—"Ya' at' ahee." They enter.

Inside, Grandfather, old Wise One, in his lawn chair lights the pipe with the end of his wrinkled finger.

RonJon: "Wow! You see that?"

Grandfather takes a big pull and exhales, the room fills with smoke. He sings a traditional shield prayer song softly with quiet drumming coming from far away.

Wild painted War Ponies prance and Eagles soar in lazy

circles rising in the smoke from his pipe.

The two boys look around in awe.

On the ceiling is the night sky, full of stars and constellations. Golden Eagle Feathers hang from stars. A dream catcher with Eagle and Hawk feathers filters the honey gold light.

Grandfather points, "Hawk for protection. Eagle for wisdom."

A sacred painted drum. A Ghost Dance Shirt decorated with scalp locks, quills and beadwork. Jars of turquoise stones. An Eagle bone breastplate and an Eagle skull.

An ancient handmade horse blanket. A saddle studded with turquoise and with brass. A handmade Indian rug. A handsome Navajo blanket on the bed. Elegant beadwork and quill work everywhere.

RonJon looks around, amazed at this mystical place: "Wow!"

Andy: "Anyway so Mom said you had a birthday present for me."

Grandfather places a bulging brain-tanned deerskin pouch in Andy's gimme hand.

Grandfather: "You and your friend. Go to the top of Sacred Vision Mountain. Dig a hole. Deep enough that when you sit, comes up to your chest."

He holds his hand to his chest to show the depth.

Grandfather: "Two holes, one for you, one for you."

He points to Andy and RonJon. "And sit in the hole. And open the pouch. There are eighteen peyote buds in that pouch. Nine for you. And nine for you."

He pokes Andy and RonJon in the stomach: "Eat them peyote buds. Consider your place in the Great Universe. Talk to the Great Spirit. He will show you the way back to your People."

Grampa sings a traditional shield prayer song softly with drumming.

Andy and RonJon look at each other...

Grandfather opens a pouch of corn pollen and sprinkles it in front of their shoes to bless their path.

Andy and RonJon drive silently up the mountain.

RonJon: "What's that over there?"

Pointing at a mountain which can be seen from far away.

Andy: "Oh, that's Shiprock. Grampa says it's sacred too."

RonJon: "He says everything's sacred."

Andy: "Yup. Pretty much. Says it's the skeleton of a giant bird."

RonJon: "Kinda would look like that if you smoke enough weed."

In the sky above the one-hundred-mile-long mountain, a

translucent vision of a huge rumbling stone pterodactyl carves a circle over the desert.

Andy: "Wanna hear something crazy?"

RonJon: "Sure."

Andy: "Grampa says the Navajo People flew here from the stars on the back of that giant bird mountain thing. Crazy huh?"

Andy and RonJon laugh—

RonJon: "Yeah, almost as crazy as a woman being made from one of a man's ribs or people walking on water, or Noah building a ark when he was four hundred years old."

Andy: "Yeah."

Andy tries to turn the truck around but cannot move the steering wheel.

Andy: "Hey, something's wrong!"

His foot on the brake pedal doesn't stop the truck.

Andy: "Crap!! NO BRAKES!!"

Fuel gauge is past empty but the truck continues to rumble upward.

RonJon: "Check out the fuel gauge."

The truck moves onward.

Andy lets go of the steering wheel.

The truck turns by itself, up the windy road.

Outlaws

Andy: "Whoa, spooky..."

Andy and RonJon's truck stops on its own on the top of the mountain and they get out.

Two shovels appear in their hands, the boys look surprised.

Andy: "Was just gonna ask how we was supposed to dig holes without no shovels."

They dig two holes side by side.

They each sit in their holes and look up at the stars.

Andy: "All's we needs in here's a coupl'a hot babes."

Andy opens the pouch and counts out nine peyote buds into RonJon's hand.

He holds nine in his.

RonJon: "What's this like?"

Andy: "Just like shrooms."

The buds glow like little radioactive uranium pillows in the twinkling starlight.

They put the peyote in their mouths and start a-chewing.

An owl hoots.

Andy and RonJon are tripped out of their minds.

An Eagle soars in the sky above.

RonJon: "Hey, look a glee gull, a p-gull, a e-gull."

Andy: "Yeah."

The Eagle swoops low over Andy and RonJon.

RonJon: "That's supposed to mean something—a sign."

Andy: "I wish I listened more to Grandfather…"

Suddenly both Andy and RonJon are covered in Eagle poop.

Elsewhere, the earth **spits** up more Indian Dead, as if popcorn.

Back on Vision Mountain, Coyotes yelp, wolves howl, bears growl, owls hoot.

Black clouds roll.

Strong cold wind blows dirt at Andy and RonJon until they are buried over their chests.

Big hard raindrops pellet them, washing away the Eagle poo.

They are so scared and cold and stoned and alone out there—they cry like little girls.

Thunder grumbles.

Rain hammers down.

Andy and RonJon are soaked to the bone and shiver in their fox holes.

A lightning bolt **spears** the ground beside them, **shakes** the earth.

They scream.

Outlaws

The earth **cracks**.

Their hair stands straight up on end.

Zig-zag furrows grow.

Dead Indians **claw** their way to the surface.

Andy and RonJon look at each other, petrified.

Skeletal Horses rise out of the ground, bellow and snort.

Two scary, partially-skeletal Indian Dead approach Ron-Jon and Andy.

Andy: "No!"

RonJon: "Go away!"

Andy: "Yeah, go away. Whatever you got we don't want."

Andy and RonJon scream bloody murder.

The Indian Dead skeletons yank RonJon and Andy out of their holes saying, "Rise up little brothers and help us reclaim the bones of our dead brothers."

RonJon and Andy look at each other, are they hallucinating?

RonJon: "Is this really happening?"

Andy: "No. Yeah. Dunno."

An Indian Dead puts two of his fingers in his mouth and whistles.

Four dead war ponies charge up.

Andy and RonJon: "Whoa!"

The Warriors leap onto their horses.

Indian Dead Warriors: "Mount up brothers and ride with us!"

RonJon and Andy stumble around, try to get up on the skeletal horses.

Indian Dead: "Ride much?"

Andy: "Oh yeah, sure, all the time."

They ride awkwardly, surrounded by screaming Indian Dead.

Andy and RonJon are freaked.

Andy's horse turns his head around and bites Andy in the leg.

Andy screams.

His scream is lost in the screaming horde of wild-riding Indian Dead.

The Tree

The pine box was too small so they chopped a hole and me feet waggled outa one end. Then they lowered me inta the ground near grandaddy. Me wife Judy cried. Me brother Norton cried. Me maw an' paw, they cried too. But me young son Jacob, he cried the loudest. An' then I heard 'em say..."Good bye."

"NO! NO! NO! I AIN'T DEAD! I AIN'T DEAD! NO I AIN'T" I holler'd, but I had no voice. But . . . it was true . . . I was dead.

Then it was quiet. It was dark. It was very dark an' very quiet for a long, long time. They came with flowers for a while, but I could not make 'em hear me words. It was dark an' quiet an' there was a lotta memories. Memories of Life.

I want'd to tell me baby son, Jacob how important every minute of Life was. How important every second of his sweet, sweet young Life was, but he heard me not. Time was once so important, but now it had no meaning at all. I drifted through eternal darkness towards forever.

Years must of blowed by like leaves in the wind. Few times, I must admit, I thought I heard music, I think, maybe. And after some time, I guess, I figger'd out how to travel a bit. How to visit. I mean, I mean, how to visit the, you know, the Living.

But I could not talk or nothing and I saw how the things that I thought was so damn important when I was alive, now they really didn't mean a damn thing. I had so much time now to think.

About all the things I should have did. All the things I should have said. All the time I wasted. How much of Life I missed strugglin' for money, as Life washed through me fingers, and flew past me like fast moving clouds above me reach, and was lost forever. But the darkness, the darkness, always the darkness surrounded me.

Me memories rattled like empty old tin cans in the darkness. But then after a while I forgave myself. And I forgave everyone else.

And then, after what must have been a long, long time, the roots, the roots, they found me. Suddenly the roots was moving all round me. Fast and quiet in the darkness. And then one wrapped round me neck.

At first I shouted: "NO. NO. NO." But it was no use. The roots they moved so quickly through the darkness, and then, after so much silence, I heard a voice. And the voice said:

"I am a Tree and now You are Me. Don't be afraid. Just let it be.

Me head had already rolled aways somewheres, so I says: "Oh . . . well . . . what the heck, I ain't got nothin' left to lose." And the roots wove through me bones, through me skeleton, found me skull an' threaded through me eye sockets and wove their hard, dark, fingers round me ribs.

And one day, the sun rose and the eternal darkness was over. An' I was the Tree.

Me leaves blowed in the wind. An' me head was in the sky. Me roots clutched to the earth, to the dark, silent earth, from where I had come. Me arms moved. An' I made sweet, sweet music with the wind in me branches.

And there was Light. Bright and shining Light. An' the bright sun it warmed me skin. An' I could see the blue, blue sky and the salty blue ocean again.

An' then one day I saw 'em lowering my sweet son Jacob into the ground. An' I sent out a root to find him.

Tugboat Thrasher

Hundred eighty-foot treasure salvage ship, *Arctic Storm*, squats at anchor off Galley Bay just south of the Queen Charlotte Islands. Three trash pumps pump steady streams of oily water from her engine hold. Captain Chuck screams into the VHF radio mike over the noisy pumps, "Tugboat *Thrasher*. Tugboat *Thrasher*. *Arctic Storm*..."

A hundred fifty miles away, nice-looking wooden fan-tail tugboat *Thrasher*, end-tied to a floating dock at sleepy little marina in Port Mellon.

Inside a cozy, varnished, wood-paneled wheelhouse, Raymond, a shiny-eyed nine-year-old sits on the lap of his tugboat captain father, Eron Knight, beside the glowing, pot-belly, cast iron, wood stove.

Captain Eron reads a story. Little Ray listens captivated.

"The evil pirate, Blackbeard, roamed the seas looking for

merchant ships to plunder. He and his cut-throat men buried their gold and loot in the sand on remote beaches. Meanwhile, off the Ivory Coast..."

Ray interrupts, "Dad, where's the Ivory Coast?"

Eron: "Somewhere off the west coast of Africa..."

The VHF radio blasts: (static...) "Tug *Thrasher*. Tug *Thrasher*. Black Creek Salvage, *Arctic Storm*. (static...) Tug *Thrasher*. *Arctic Storm*. Channel 16. Capt'n—you on this side?" (static...)

Eron: "Sounds like somebody needs our help, I'll read to you more later." He puts the book down, carries Ray to his little bunk near the wheel, tucks him in under the covers.

Ray: "But Dad, it's way early for bed..."

Eron picks up the mike: "Go 'head *Arctic Storm*."

On the radio: (static) "Capt'n Eron, let's go six-eight. Six-eight."

Eron turns the radio knob to 68.

VHF radio: (static) "Capt'n Eron, *Arctic Storm;* takin' on water off of Watson's Bay. Prop shaft's broke, stern tube's tore out."

Eron: "Taking on how much water?"

VHF: "More'n two thousand gallons a hour."

Eron looks at little Ray.

Ray smiles.

44

VHF radio: "Can you run up here an' tow us down to the shipyard over at Ballard?"

Eron looks at Ray.

Ray goes thumbs up.

Ray: "Which one's *Arctic Storm?*"

Eron: "Treasure boat; big black mailbox hangin' off the back. Was working a legendary wreck off Galleon Bay. Looking for that Spanish Galleon, supposed to been sunk by pirates off there in the sixteen hundreds full of gold— nobody never found nothin'..."

Ray: "I remember her. Big gnarly-looking blue one."

Eron: "That's the one. A good four-day job. Might be the last big one b'fore you go back to school. Should we do it?"

Ray: "What the heck, Dad. He won't stiff us, will he?"

Eron shakes his head no.

He keys the mike. "Okay, *Arctic Storm*. Eight-fifty. Me and my best mate can leave right away." Eron winks at Ray. "Got 'nough pumps?"

VHF radio: (static) "Wouldn't hurt t' bring one 'r two more. Hurry and...be careful."

Eron: "Always."

Eron turns and looks at Ray...both go thumbs up.

OCEAN—LATE AFTERNOON

Thrasher, covered in spray, plows into the lumpy knuckles of the Northwest Pacific.

ONSHORE—Ruggedly spectacular coastline. Rocky shore. Thick, lush rainforests. Black bears eat berries, and look up as Tugboat *Thrasher* steams past. An eagle dives, rips a wriggling silvery salmon from the dark water.

TUGBOAT THRASHER—UNDERWAY—SUNSET

Bangs headlong into the waves, heads north, plowing into a nasty, cold, gray ocean...

WHEEL HOUSE—NIGHT

Little Ray at the wooden wheel, holds her on the compass. Eron beside him finishes splicing a thimble into the hawser (tow rope).

Eron: "How's the oil pressure?"

Ray: "Seventy pounds."

Eron: "Temperature?"

Ray: "One seven-five."

Eron: "Good, good..."

Eron lifts the double-sided ax from the holder on the bulkhead, puts it in the vise. He pulls out a metal file, files one side.

Eron: "Here's how you sharpen an ax. File it till there's a burr then..."

Ray (imitates his father's voice), "Flip her over an' file off the burr."

THRASHER—LATER—NIGHT

Thrasher approaches a wooded peninsula. Ray at the wheel. Eron coils the hawser in a figure-eight on the stern deck, walks back to the wheelhouse, leans in through the door.

Ray: "Should be just up ahead 'bout two miles, Dad."

Tug *Thrasher's* running lights appear in the dark around the bend of the peninsula. Ray at the wheel. *Thrasher* comes alongside *Arctic Storm*. Eron tosses lines. *Arctic Storm* deckhands, Blue and Malborne tie up *Thrasher*. Ray turns on towing lights—white light over a white. Eron jumps aboard *Arctic Storm*. He greets Blue and Malborne shouting over the noisy pumps, "Hey."

Blue shouts, "How ya doin' Cap?"

Eron shouts, "Just two of you?"

Malborne shouts, "Yup. Second shift crew. Others got off. Check it out..."

Blue opens the engine room door. Shines a flashlight to show Eron the damage.

Eron drags his two pumps onboard. Malborne and Blue get them running. Eron's flashlight lights up blood on the deck.

Eron: "Where's the blood from?" He shines the flashlight along the blood trail to the galley...

Malborne looks away, then back at Eron. "Oh, the cook. Cook cut his ah... hand. Had to get tooken off to the hospital up in Powell River."

Eron shines the light in the galley window, into the darkness. He looks Malborne in the eye. Eron knows Malborne's lying, knows something bad must have happened here. He steps up to the foredeck, secures a chain bridle to *Arctic Storm's* bow and shackles the tow hawser to the middle of the chain.

Eron: "Okay, go get the anchor up."

Blue winches up *Arctic Storm's* anchor. Eron climbs back aboard Tug *Thrasher*. Blue and Malborne untie *Trasher*.

THRASHER—UNDERWAY—NIGHT

Little Ray eases *Thrasher* ahead into the darkness, real slow. Eron at the fantail feeds out the tow hawser through the rollers. One of the rollers jams. Eron pokes it, then pries at it with a crow bar and frees it up.

ARCTIC STORM IN TOW—NIGHT

STERN DECK—Blue and Malborne shackle long lines to each big steel salvage box. They secure a large round red buoy to the end of each line so they can retrieve the boxes after *Arctic Storm* sinks. They stop the pumps.

THRASHER—NIGHT

Through the red glow of the wheelhouse front windows—Ray at the wheel. Eron makes entry in ship's log. *Thrasher* displays running lights and towing lights: red to left, green to right, white behind, and on the stubby tug mast—white over white when towing at night.

ARCTIC STORM—In tow 300 feet behind Tug *Thrasher*. Starry sky above.

Blue and Malborne untie *Meatball*, a thirty-foot workboat hip-tied to *Arctic Storm's* port, they jump aboard and get underway as *Arctic Storm* sinks; the cold black ocean gulps her down...

TUG THRASHER—UNDERWAY

Suddenly, *Thrasher's* stern is violently pulled underwater with such force it knocks Eron backwards against the wheelhouse bulkhead. He looks out through the aft window. Half of *Thrasher's* stern deck is underwater; tugboat captain's worst nightmare. *Arctic Storm* nowhere in sight; tow hawser, straight down.

He shouts to Ray, "Take her outta gear!"

Eron grabs a safety harness and the sharp ax. Charges out the wheelhouse buckling on his harness. He knows what he has to do and that it won't be easy.

Thrasher's stern comes shooting up into the air, eight, ten feet out of the water. Eron crouches to his knees, chops the hawser at the tow bitts with the ax. But the hawser does not run free, it is jammed in the twisted stern roller. *Thrasher's* stern gets sucked down underwater again.

UNDERWATER

At the end of the tow hawser—sunken *Arctic Storm* —her bow bounces on the rocky bottom.

TUG THRASHER—DRIFTING

Eron, safety harness clipped to the bitts, hangs on as *Thrasher's* stern heaves up into the air. Water cascades off him as the stern deck shoots upwards again.

Mangled stern rollers trap the hawser, he chops at the tow rope with the ax, crazy with adrenalin. Whack! Whack! Whack!

The ax chops half-way through, strikes the steel roller; sparks fly.

Thrasher's stern goes underwater again. Eron crouches, holds on tight. *Thrasher's* stern shoots straight up into the air again. Water cascading. Eron chops completely through the hawser. The stern comes smashing back down.

The tugboat shudders and rocks. Eron sits and gasps for air on the stern deck. Stands, soaked, exhausted, unbuckles the safety harness, carries the ax back into the wheelhouse.

Eron: "You all right son?" Ray's eyes wide.

Ray: "Yeah, Dad. Wow! You okay?"

Eron: "Yeah."

Meatball approaches. Eron lumbers back out on deck.

Meatball close. The red buoy suddenly shoots up into the air, and lands floating between *Meatball* and *Thrasher* with a violent dispatch of big noisy bubbles.

MEATBALL—DRIFTING—NIGHT

Blue shines a spotlight on the red buoy and then on Eron. Malborne pulls out the shotgun and fires on Eron. **Bam!** Eron goes down—he's hit! Malborne pumps four rounds into wheelhouse. **Bam! Bam! Bam! Bam!** Hot lead spits out. Windows explode in a shower of glass. Ray ducks low.

Tugboat *Thrasher*, lights out, drifts away into darkness.

Malborne holds a boat hook and fishes the red buoy out of the water. He pulls the line up to the bow. Wraps it around the anchor winch wildcat. Malborne throws the lever, pulls up the line. The noisy winch groans, slows as it takes the full weight. Blue moves forward.

Malborne strains. He tails the line as the winch begins to pull up the sunken, heavy, iron salvage box. Malborne yells, "We'll catch up to the tug and make sure they're all dead. Then we'll sink 'em too. First we get this box up."

Blue yells, "Where... where's the other float?"

Malborne: "Musta fouled on the wreck. Mark this spot on the GPS." Blue turns to go to the wheelhouse.

Outlaws

Suddenly, out of the pitch-dark night, here comes Tug-boat *Thrasher's* big black bow. 300 Tons; 2,500 snorting locomotive 6-110 Detroit diesel horsepower. Moving full-speed ahead. Big foamy bow wake. Plowing right for *Meatball*.

Through the red glow of *Thrasher's* wheelhouse instruments, little Ray at the wheel. His eyes full of fire—his teeth clenched.

Malborne looks up at *Thrasher's* bow. His right hand fouls between the rope and winch. And is severed off at the wrist. Blood shoots out... he yells, "MY HAND!" just as *Thrasher's* bow T-bones *Meatball's* port midship. *Meatball* rolls over on its starboard side in a shower of noisy, splintering wood and *Meatball* is not-so-neatly cut in half.

Little Ray drives *Thrasher* right through *Meatball* and out the other side. He takes *Thrasher* out of gear. He hugs his father who has dragged himself back to Ray and now lies on the wheelhouse floor. Eron cuts his pants and examines his wounded leg with a flashlight.

Ray: "Daddy. Your leg!"

Bleeding bad, Eron rips off his shirt, rolls it up and fastens a tourniquet around his thigh.

Eron: "I'll be okay, son".

Ray: "You sure, Dad?"

Eron: "Just a (wince) scratch, son."

Ray: "Guess we're not gonna get paid for this tow job now."

Eron: "Nope. Not this one or the two pumps." Eron smiles and takes a big breath.

Ray: "This is the first time we ever lost a tow and drove the *Thrasher* through another boat all in the same day."

Eron: "By the way... who taught you how to drive like that?"

Ray: "You, Dad." Both laugh and clunk knuckles. "Will the Coast Guard Auxiliary make us give back our safe boating award now?" They laugh.

Ray puts *Thrasher* into gear and leans on the throttle. But *Thrasher* moves sluggishly. The bow is low and bounces up and down. Eron looks at Ray...

Eron: "Now what?"

Eron limps out of the wheelhouse and up the foredeck. He leans on the bow rail to have a look over the side and shines a flashlight at the other big red buoy and a line caught behind the Turks head, (the lower bow fender).

Eron: "Something caught on the Turk's head... a line with a red buoy."

Ray helps Eron pull the line up to the deck with a boat hook. Eron loosens the tourniquet. Waits a few seconds and tightens it up again. He wraps the rope round the midship winch, through a snatch-block and pulls on the winch lever.

He attaches a boom to the rope. Swings the boom outboard. Winches up the big iron salvage box. Swings it onto the deck.

THRASHER—DRIFTING—OFFSHORE

Eron lights up an acetylene torch and cut-torches open the big steel box. Eron and Ray lean over the edge and look inside...at two hundred shiny gold bars from the sunken wreck *Arctic Storm* salvaged!

Eron picks up one and hands it to Ray who almost drops it. Ray: "Can we bury it in the sand, just like Blackbeard?"

Eron: "Where?"

Ray: "In the sandbox in the backyard, Dad."

BACKYARD—NIGHT

Little Ray pats the last shovelful of sand on the sandbox. He carries the shovel to Eron. They plant a tree nearby. Eron reaches up with one hand to show Ray that the tree will be huge.

Eron: "When you grow up this'll be a giant tree."

"It's peaceful here."

They listen to the quiet and look up at the silent twinkling universe.

Thrasher, Part Two— If a Tree Can Talk

Twenty years later. Eron and Ray are dead and buried under the tree in the backyard. Ray's wife, Sarah, lives in Eron's house with her daughter and son.

ERON'S HOUSE—PACIFIC NORTHWEST— MORNING FOG—BACK PORCH

Jennifer, an angelic little girl with wild curls stands behind a screen door that faces a backyard.

"Mom?"

Mom, in the kitchen, her back to Jennifer.

"Mom?"

"Yes, Angel?"

Outlaws

We see there is something wrong with Jennifer's eyes.

"If you're blind?..."

Jennifer's mom stops washing dishes, dries her hands, turns to face her, she looks at her hands.

"Yes?"

"If you're blind, do you think you can ever learn to really see with your ears?"

Her mother holds her hands over her eyes, a mercurial tear glides down her cheek.

"Why did daddy leave, mom?"

Mom puts her hands over her mouth. She turns her back and continues washing dishes. "Not now, please, Jennifer... I just can't do this..."

"Was it because of me?"

No answer.

"Did he leave because of me?"

Jennifer opens the screen door, her hurt, searching whisper floats out into the backyard.

In the backyard, a Tree.

A bird sings a complex set of notes.

We watch Jennifer's lips as she whistles the bird's soulful song, note for note.

A dust-devil shivers a chain swing.

Thrasher, Part II, If a Tree Can Talk

A sandbox.

A fence and beyond...

Verdant distant miles of time roll backward through seasons' greenest hills and majestic trees, to an ocean, through eerie lifting fog, to a remote coastline where Tug-boat *Thrasher* pounds into the white knuckles of the great Pacific Ocean.

On the street at Jennifer's house a dirty, dark green pick-up truck parks, motor running.

The driver, minus his right hand, holds binoculars to his eyes, looks over the fence into the back yard, to a Tree with a swing and a sandbox.

Jennifer's brother, freckle-faced Stevie Knight, nine, wears a baseball cap backwards, sails like a demon through the air under the Tree on the creaking swing.

Leaves glide from the big Tree on a light breeze.

Late summer sun warms Jennifer's grandfather's small, '50s vintage cottage.

We watch through the screen door as Jennifer Knight talks to her Mom.

Their voices float into the backyard.

"Mom, when do you think daddy will come back home?"

Sarah is caught off-guard... her back to Jennifer, she bites her lower lip, closes her eyes for a second and looks back at Jennifer.

"Not now, go outside and play, little angel."

"But you *never* talk about him... Didn't daddy love me?"

"Jennifer! Not now, Jennifer, please!"

Jennifer, her back to her mother, stands behind the screen door, looks with blind eyes out into the backyard...

The screen door creaks open. Jennifer steps outside. She turns toward the fence, to the street, to the dark green truck.

This is where we see Jennifer's eyes again. Her eyelids flutter like a dying butterfly...

We are snapped back to awkward reality by Stevie on the swing

"Push Me!"

Jennifer's hand reaches beside the door for her cane. The end of the thin, white cane hovers on familiar air. Above the porch, it feels for and taps the edge of the top step. She walks carefully down the stairs.

The cane tip floats into the backyard, feels the air, not for what is, but what might be. The backyard is her whole world, her white shoes weightless in the thick green grass.

At the Tree, she lifts her hand. Fingertips half-inch from Tree trunk, hovering, feeling. A profound private sensitivity between Tree and fingertip—lingering there for a moment—feeling.

"Push Me!"

Jennifer smiles at the Tree and passes.

"Push Me! Push Me! Push Me!"

By the breeze on her face. By the creaking of chain. The sound of the wind on Stevie's body. She feels the perimeter of his energy arc and steps towards the edge of that arc, lays down her cane. When her hands come up, they're on his back. She pushes her brother. He rockets higher and higher. Jennifer steps back.

"Faster, slave! Faster! Push Me Faster!"

She turns to the Tree. Bends down. Picks up her cane and moves. Pulled to the Tree by unseen hooks of magnetism. A late summer breeze strains its fingers through her hair and rustles her summer dress, pressing it against her frail body.

She stops. Kneels. Lies on her back. Looks up at the Tree with eyes that cannot see what we can see:

Curvy branches hug the sky, shimmering leaves filter a rushing river of wind, a field of snowy clouds.

Now we see what Jennifer sees:

A blur of shape, an abstract painting, an undulating pyramid of light, the painting of a mad, tortured impressionist, beauty without form, form without definition.

Behind the screen door, Jennifer's mom watches her. She whispers a prayer through tears. "Dear God, please, please be kind to her. Dear God, please... watch over her, please... help her..."

Outlaws

Jennifer to the tree, "You are so beautiful."

She listens to soft Tree sounds. She sits down on the knuckle of a big root, moves her head close to the Tree. Her little ear touches rough bark. Trunk towers. Branches, leaves rake the blue, blue sky. The wind whispers through the leaves.

Tree limbs softly moan—sounds of green and golden amber sap—of dreams of bird and insect. She inhales the Tree scent. Fingertips on Tree bark...

"I *wish* you could talk..."

Eerie sound of the wind. Leaves rustle. Branches creak...

"I really, really, really wish you could talk... I... I really need... a friend..."

Stevie looks back to see why his sister isn't pushing anymore. Sees her pressing her ear to a tree. Drags his foot to stop. Gets off the swing. Dust rising, he stomps up to her. "What are *you* doing?"

"Sshh. I'm listening to the Tree."

"Give me a break... You're psycho..."

"Shhh... the Tree is going to talk...listen..."

Stevie leans in and puts his ear against the Tree bark...

"I don't hear nothin', you weirdo."

Stevie runs back to the house. Swing still swinging.

On the porch, the screen door squeaks open. Stevie scoots inside. Screen door squeaks and slams shut.

"Mom, my retard sister's talking to trees again."

Stevie runs through the house, super-fast. And out the front door. He sprints silently alongside the house to the backyard. He quietly sneaks up to the far side of the Tree.

Jennifer's ear against Tree bark. She puts her arms around the Tree. Little fingers spread. She hugs the Tree, "I love you." Leaves crackle. "Please talk to me."

Stevie crouches on the other side of the Tree. Hand over his mouth to suppress a giggle. In his deepest voice: "I a m   a   t r e e. I a m a t r e e... a n d   y o u   a r e... a ... a psycho moron. "

Jennifer gets up. Her hand bumps on bark as she marches around the Tree. She kicks her brother's foot.

"You little creep!"

Stevie jumps away and skips back to the house with his hand over his mouth, giggling. He leaps up the porch steps. The screen door screeches, and slams shut.

Jennifer takes four steps away from the Tree. She sits on the wooden rim of the sandbox. Her toes in sand. Her back to the Tree. The Tree moans softly, leaves whisper to the wind...

A ray of golden light bathes Jennifer in an unnatural glow.

"Jennifer? Jennifer? Come in here. Your dinner's getting cold."

Jennifer gets up, brushes herself off, she puts her fingertips on the Tree again. "I'll be back... I promise."

She smiles at the Tree, picks up her cane and feels her way back toward the house as leaves flicker in the wind, then the sound of the screen door closing.

"Jennifer, what were you doing out there?"

"I was listening to the Tree; the Tree was going to talk to me."

"Jennifer, trees don't talk. Now please, eat your dinner. You too, Stevie."

On the street, the green pickup rolls past the house.

Jennifer sits down at the table. "Mom, someone was watching our house across the street in an old Ford truck."

Sarah drops a fork... "How could you possibly know that?"

"I heard the motor running. Old Fords, the gears kinda grind, and whir... I could... I could feel someone was watching."

Mom walks into the kitchen. "I just don't know, I can't tell anymore when you're telling the truth or making things up."

Stevie kicks Jennifer's leg. "You're such a little psycho liar."

Mom moves the curtains in the kitchen and looks out the window at the empty street. She comes back and puts a hot dinner casserole on the table.

"Mom, can I sleep over at Kevin's Friday night?"

"If it's okay with Kevin's mom, Stevie."

"Uhh huh, it's okay with her."

Mom walks back to the kitchen.

Stevie whispers to Jennifer. "You lie so much you don't even have any friends. You're such a freakazoid. Why couldn't I have had a normal brother instead of you?"

Jennifer turns her head away from Stevie, toward the screen door, toward the Tree in the backyard.

Behind the Tree, fiery colors blowtorch the darkening sky. A sulfurous yellow moon glows through the leaves.

Jennifer looks with blind eyes out into the obtuse darkness at the Tree and presses her small hands against the screen.

NEXT MORNING

The Green pickup truck parks across the street. Malborne looks into backyard with binoculars.

Jennifer stands inside the screen door. "I'm going outside to play now. That Ford truck is back."

"What did you say, Angel?"

"The truck is back, he's watching us."

Sarah wipes the last dish.

The green pickup truck drives away.

Sarah wipes her hands, spreads the curtains and looks out the window at the street. The truck is gone.

Outlaws

Jennifer opens the creaky screen door. She walks out onto the wooden porch, into the yellow sunshine. She stops and turns toward the Tree.

Jennifer picks up her cane, steps carefully down each stair.

She moves to the Tree, curls blowing; her summer dress wafts in the breeze. She turns her head up at the Tree. She sits on a twisted root and whispers to the Tree, "I wish I were a tree. Then everything would be perfect. I wouldn't be blind, all I'd have to do is be a tree; why am I even alive? You think I like being this way? Why? Why did this happen to me? Why couldn't I be like everyone else? Why are other kids so lucky? Why can't I see?"

Her head raises slowly, "Can trees see? Tell me!... Tell me!... Say something! If you care at all... Say something! Say something or I'll never talk to you again."

Wind blows. Dead leaves spiral downward. A big gray cloud sails in front of the sun. Rain falls from the sky. Jennifer's getting wet, she sneezes. She picks up her cane and sloshes back to the house.

Later, the sun's out. Jennifer steps down each stair, the tip of her cane tapping. She moves to the Tree. She carries a hat box. She opens the box and feels the different colored ribbons. Then she takes out a spool and ties a purple ribbon around the tree in a perfect bow.

She sits down on a boney root.

Her grandfather Eron's ghost face stretches the bark,

presses out and looks down on Jennifer.

She pulls her curly, long, strands away from her ear, moves close to the Tree. Her ear touches the Tree. Jennifer listens to Tree sounds. Above her, the Ghost Face disappears inside the Tree.

A distant freight train whistle blows. She picks up her cane and moves toward the porch. The screen door squeaks open and slams shut.

In the backyard, the boy from the tugboat, Jennifer's father Ray, pushes part-way out of the Tree. His ghost head cranes looking from side to side, looking for his daughter, for his sweet blind Jennifer. He tries to call out to her but cannot make words or sounds.

The ghost of his father, tugboat *Thrasher's* Captain Eron—Jennifer's grandfather—pushes out of the Tree, puts his arm around his son and pulls him back into the Tree.

Wind rustles leaves.

Branches creak and groan as the wind strengthens.

Jennifer sleeps in her pink bedroom. In her dream she sees her father, Ray, as a boy. He stands over the sandbox, shoveling sand into a hole, burying something... He hands his father the shovel.

Next morning, Jennifer dresses fast. In the backyard she moves to the back of the garage. Picks up a shovel. Carries the shovel to the sandbox. She digs in the center of the sandbox. The Tree towers over her. She digs and digs, piling sand neatly beside the sandbox. Then her shovel clunks on something hard. She puts down the shovel and digs with her hands, sand flying. She uncovers the top of a shiny gold brick. She pushes the sand away from the edges and pries out the gold bar. She lifts it out and puts it down on the wooden edge of the sandbox. It gleams.

She shovels the sand back over the hole and pads it down with her feet. She puts the shovel away. And goes up the porch steps, props the screen door open with a flowerpot. She moves back to the sandbox. With all her strength, Jennifer picks up the heavy gold brick and carries it from the sandbox toward the house using her toes as a cane.

In the street, the pickup parks across from Jennifer's house. Malborne looks through binoculars. He sees Jennifer carrying the gold brick. And puts down the binoculars. He slides a .45 Magnum out from under the seat and grins. He opens the glove box, takes out a silencer cylinder.

Holding the pistol between his knees he carefully threads it onto the end of the gun. He holds the gun with his left hand. Aims at Jennifer. Little Jennifer's chest is in the sights. Then moves it to aim at the telephone wires where they attach to the front of the house and pulls the trigger—Poot! —misses. Pulls the trigger again—Poot! —misses again. He steadies the gun with his stump. Pulls the trigger again—Poot! —shoots off the telephone wire, it falls to the lawn.

He blows out the smoke from the end of the gun, puts it

in his jacket pocket and gets out of the pickup. He looks both ways, nobody outside any of the houses, no cars. He walks across the street.

He jumps the fence into the backyard. The big Tree shivers.

Malborne looks around.

The screen door is propped open with a flowerpot. He sticks his left hand into his pocket on the gun. Sneaks over to the porch, up the stairs and in through the open screen door.

Malborne pulls out his gun, sneaks silently across the living room, hides behind a wall. He peeks out around the corner. Sarah's back is to Jennifer as she carries the heavy gold bar. Wild eyes flashing, he puts the warm gun to his lips and kisses it.

"Hey Mom, look at this!"

Sarah turns around and she drops a coffee can. It rolls across the floor.

"Jennifer! What on earth...?"

She realizes immediately what it is, it's so shiny, it can only be one thing.

"Where did you get that?"

Malborne steps out with his gun behind his back. "That's a very good question."

"Who are you? What are you doing in my house?"

She pushes Jennifer behind her and grabs the phone. No dial tone. Malborne aims the gun at little Jennifer's head.

"Where did you find that?"

Sarah shields her with her body, "Jennifer, don't say anything to him."

Just then the front door opens. Jennifer's brother Stevie marches in, "Hi, Mom, I'm home. What you got to eat?"

He freezes when he sees Malborne standing with the gun pointed at Jennifer and his mom.

"Close the door, kid. Come in."

Stevie shuts the door, moves up close to his Mom.

The doorbell rings. They all look at the door.

The doorbell rings again.

Malborne scowls, "Don't answer that."

The doorbell rings again. The door opens. Becky, Sarah's neighbor leans in, "Sarah, it's me, Becky. Yoo hooo! Are you here? Yoo hoo!"

"Don't answer." He points the gun at each of them.

Jennifer drops the gold bar with a loud clank!

Malborne's trigger finger twitches at the noise. His gun goes off. Poot! A bullet slams a hole in the kitchen wall above them. Plaster and bits of wood rain down on Jennifer's Mom, Stevie, and Jennifer.

Becky, "Sarah, I tried to call, but your phone wasn't working,

I wanted you to meet my uncle, the seventh circuit judge."

Malborne mutters, "Damn!"

Becky walks into the kitchen with Judge Johnson. They freeze when they see Malborne standing there holding the silenced gun.

Becky and the Judge look at Sarah standing with Jennifer and Stevie on either side, covered in white plaster dust.

The Judge sees the big bullet hole in the kitchen wall, just above Jennifer's Mom's head. "What's the meaning of this?"

Malborne points the gun at them—"Shut up! Get over there with the others." He waggles the gun toward Sarah, Stevie, and Jennifer.

Becky: "Who are you?"

"You shut up. Now Jennifer, one more time. Where did you get the gold?"

"In the backyard."

"Where in the backyard?"

"I can show you."

Malborne waggles the gun toward the backdoor, "Okay, everybody, out the back door and nobody try anything funny."

Door bell rings.

Malborne scowls, "Shit!

Stevie: "Shouldn't swear, Mister..."

In walks the telephone man. "Hello. Excuse me, I was just driving down Pacific and I saw my telephone line lying across your front..."

Then he sees Jennifer, Sarah, Stevie, Becky and the Judge all standing together with their hands up.

Across the room Malborne points the big gun at the phone man.

Becky huffs, "When *my* phone stops working, it takes me four days to get a repair man."

Malborne, "Shut up! Everybody. Shut up! Out the back door. Now!"

Everyone walks out the back door. The six captives march down the porch stairs into the backyard with their hands up.

"All of you, stand against that tree. Do it! Do it now!" He wags his gun.

They all move over to the Tree. He sees some rope hanging near the shovel, beside the garage. He side-steps to the rope. And tosses it to the telephone man. "Now put your hands down. Tie them all up to the tree." He points the gun at the phone man. "Do it or die Phone Man!"

He fires the gun up in the air. Poot! Poot!

Two bullets hit a tree limb. Leaves and bark scatter down onto the six standing under the tree. They duck and cover their heads with their hands.

"Do it now!"

The phone man ties the others to the tree.

Just then the back screen door opens with a screech. It's Stevie's little friend, Kevin. "Can Stevie come over to my house to play?"

Malborne yells, "No!"

Stevie: "You're an asshole, mister."

Sarah: "Watch your language young man!"

Kevin: "What's going on Stevie? Are you all playing a game?"

Malborne: "Shut up, kid. Over there, against the tree." He waggles the gun.

"Can I stand next to Stevie?"

"Okay. But shut up! Go ahead, tie them up."

Phone man wraps the rope around the six and around the tree.

"Now, tie yourself up too; wrap it around yourself, tie a knot and squeeze under the ropes too."

The phone man wraps himself up. He slithers in under the rope.

"Now, Jennifer. Where exactly did you find that gold? Show me!"

Jennifer shakes her head, "Not telling."

Outlaws

"You better tell me or I'll shoot your mom first, and then your brother and then Becky and the Judge and the other kid just for fun—where's the gold?"

He moves up close to Jennifer. Bends down so that he's eye-to-eye with her. Strokes her hair with the stump of his right hand, touches her face with it.

Jennifer turns away and cries out, "Leave me *alone*."

Malborne continues to touch her face, neck and chest with his stump.

Stevie wiggles to free himself but it's no use.

"Leave my sister alone you creep!"

Stevie frees his leg and kicks Malborne hard. "Leave her alone! Leave her alone!"

Malborne hits Stevie in the head with the silencer of his gun.

Sarah: "Stevie!"

Malborne pins Jennifer's small hand against the tree with the gun. "Tell me or I'll make your hand look just like mine!" He rubs his disfigured stump against her face.

Jennifer's mom: "Tell him, Jennifer. Tell him. It's okay. Tell him."

Jennifer turns her head. "In the sandbox. Get away from me. I'm sorry, I'm sorry Mom."

"It's okay, Jennifer."

Malborne side-steps over to the garage. Picks up the shovel.

He side-steps to the sandbox. He puts the gun in his pocket, jams his right stump through the shovel handle and starts digging.

Stevie wiggles, trying to get untied.

Malborne jams the shovel into the sand pulls out his pistol and fires two more shots. They hit the same Tree limb, again bits of bark rain down. "Now stay still or the next bullet's for you." He digs and digs and digs and digs.

The Tree begins to tremble faintly at first, almost imperceptibly. But Jennifer notices first, and sniffles.

The Tree shakes a little stronger.

The others notice it now and turn to look up at the Tree.

The Tree shakes more and more.

The roots shake; the ground shakes harder and harder each time the shovel hits the sand.

Becky, the Judge, Stevie, Kevin, the Phone Man, Jennifer and Sarah all look at each other.

All around—everything is shaking.

With a resonating ring, Malborne's shovel hits something hard. Malborne is oblivious to the tremors which match the greedy heartbeat pounding in his head. He throws down the shovel and kneels. He digs frantically with his stump and his left hand and stops when he sees the shiny gold. He digs around the gold bars that pave the bottom of the sandbox.

Outlaws

The earth now heaves violently, like a major earthquake.

Dogs bark; birds take flight; cats screech.

Suddenly, a loud snap above: the branch that the five bullets hit. It splinters as it breaks away from the Tree and crashes through the air. Oblivious, Malborne wedges out a gold brick. He's drooling. He picks it up and blows the sand off it just as the big branch falls on him and pins him down, traps him like a cockroach under a boot. He cannot move.

The earth shakes gently now.

Jennifer turns her head and kisses the Tree.

The Healer— Shepherd Girl

REMOTE AFGHANISTAN LANDSCAPE

Wind blows endless clouds of doomful dust. A US Marine convoy. The ghostlike roar of mechanical dinosaurs, brown like the dust through which they advance.

Trucks, Humvees, tankers full of diesel fuel, canvas-covered troop trucks, and various other armored vehicles lumber through the village of rough houses, broken windows, piles of brick and stone where buildings once stood carrying the sticky smell of cosmoline, diesel, gunpowder, and the putrid urn of death.

Afghans, silent, apprehensive, watch from the street. Children dressed in ragged clothes cower behind mothers, heads covered, dark eyes weary, frightened as the uninvited circus of monsters rumbles past. Crushing stones, they crawl over the rocky road.

Marines, bandanas over their noses and mouths, look blandly through the dust as they shake and bounce in their vehicles.

An Afghan man wearing a red shirt, and his teenage son hold an improvised sign that reads: "THAMK YUO AMERICA"

A Marine points to the sign with the butt of his rifle, "Don't trust any of 'em."

Jack Yahzee, Navajo, recently deployed from the Albuquerque National Guard, long hair, no rifle, no gun; now a Navy Corpsman, field medic—rides shotgun, bounces, organizes his first-aid bag.

The Driver throws the Red Shirt Guy thumbs-up, gets a thumbs-up in return. The convoy snakes along. Dust rising.

Buildings and ruins give way to rugged desert terrain. The trucks labor slow, gears whining, over ruts and rocks.

An I.E.D. (Improvised Explosive Device) detonates under one of the trucks. The back end of the truck lifts off the ground. When the truck comes crashing down, it lands on its side with a bone-breaking thump, dust cloud rising.

The convoy stops. Random artillery fire. Marine Snipers dismount, fire automatic weapons as they rush nearby rocks looking for insurgents. A Marine wildly lobs a frag grenade. It lands on the other side of some big boulders and explodes.

The soldiers wait for more fire to define insurgents' positions.

A Humvee off-roads kicking up dust. A Marine runs out, two Marines covering him, back to back, nervously sighting their rifles; the Marine attaches a winch hook to the truck lying on its side. The truck is winched upright with a shudder. Near the front of the convoy comes the call, "Corpsman up! Corpsman up!"

Jack moves like a hot piston, barreling along, loaded down with first aid bag and heavy backpack. A hail of spitting bullets and sweet thick black smoke darkens the air. Jack charges along the line of trucks. Shells rip into the vehicles as he runs, and thud into his backpack.

Another I.E.D. detonates. Jack feels a chunk of hot shrapnel rip past his leg. With a limp, but barely slowing, thinking: *somewhere out there a wounded Marine needs me.*

American Soldiers engage in return fire. Jack reaches the dented truck. He heaves open the door. A Marine with serious facial wounds and a big red hole in his left arm grunts, "Help me! Oh God! I can't see. Help me..." Jack eases him to the ground.

More live fire. He turns the soldier on his side and pushes a rubber hose into what's left of his nose so he can breathe. Two soldiers run up with a backboard. Three more provide cover fire, shielding Jack with their bodies, firing random bursts. They know Jack'd be there for them.

Jack yanks a tourniquet under the soldier's armpit, cranks round and jams the end of the aluminum rod under the tight rubber tubing.

Jack: "Okay, ready. Go! Go!" They load the wounded on the stretcher and run with it to an armored vehicle. Two Marines alongside provide cover, firing bullets nonstop.

They slide the wounded man into the back of the truck. An old-style pineapple grenade hits the windshield and rolls down to the hood. Jack and two Marines freeze. But the dud grenade doesn't go off.

Jack hooks up I.V. and injects the soldier with morphine, "You're gonna be alright."

Another I.E.D. goes off. BAM!

A soldier watches Jack work. Jack instructs him, "Hold this. Keep pressure on the wound here and here."

Jack bails, slaps the side of the truck with his hand. "Go! Go!" The driver u-turns back, dust rising behind the vehicle.

Jack's pant leg bright red with blood. Another marine shouts, "Corpsman up!" Jack eyeballs the long line of trucks. He runs to a fallen Marine whose entire front is soaked in dark blood.

One Marine kneels beside him, two more, with weapons, stand guard providing cover fire. Jack knifes open the wounded Marine's tattered frag vest. A sucking sound with foaming blood gurgles out a ragged hole the size of a cell phone in his chest.

Jack carefully rolls him on his side, sees the exit wound on his back. He wipes away blood, sticks a pressure bandage over the exit hole and turns him on his back again. He tries to hold the chest wound together with another pressure bandage. But there's too much blood.

Jack works quickly; he won't give up this Marine. "I got you. Hang on. I got you." But air-filled bubbles of blood leak between Jack's fingers from punctured lungs.

The wounded Marine grabs Jack's arm and whispers, "Give me my weapon." Jack puts the M4 in his hand. Wounded Marine: "Semper..." and dies. Jack whispers to him, "Fi"

Three Marine shooters rush a ruined building toward insurgent fire. One hand signals, "You, go round that way. You, that way."

One Marine sneaks up behind two Insurgents with a rocket launcher on a tripod—(they are the man with the red shirt and his teenage son with the "thamk yuo" sign.)

The Marine shoots the father. The boy, crying gets on his knees, puts his hands behind his head. The Marine shoots the boy. Father and son dead on the ground on top of each other, blood mixing with blood.

The convoy grinds onward along washboard ruts. The

trucks halt for a little girl who herds a few skinny sheep across the road. The sheep stop.

Lead truck driver leans out, signals to get the sheep the fuck off the road. Honks the horn.

From tall grass on either side comes rifle fire and rocket-propelled grenades.

Lead truck driver Marine is hit. He clutches his shoulder and screams.

The little shepherd girl freezes in front of the truck; she is paralyzed with fear.

A Marine in the lead truck raises his rifle and points it at her heart. His buddy pushes the rifle down as he pulls the trigger.

The sheep scatter. The little shepherd girl runs away with her sheep.

From trucks, Marines return fire, M203 Grenade Launchers blow random blast into grass.

Night: Bombs fall from the air and explode in random bursts below.

A quiet morning in Silver Spring MD. A black Ford SUV with government tags glides to a stop on a leafy street in front of a white plastic picket fence.

Two military officers get out. They straighten their spotless uniforms, and spray breath mint in their mouths. A flop-ear bunny hops across the perfect grass lawn. Big Stars and Stripes flapping on the flagpole in the safe suburban breeze.

They head for the white plastic, stain-resistant front door.

In American ammunition factories, thousands and thousands of newly-made bombs ride endless conveyor belts. Freight trains clack down iron rails, stacked with bombs and tanks.

Bombs are loaded into cargo bays of B-2 bombers.

More endless rows of bombs rumble along conveyor belts.

Dark sky. US bombs drop silently from the belly of bombers like eggs from giant fish. The bombs float quietly, gracefully through the black starry sky. They explode in thunderous orchestrated earth-shaking orange blossoms of fire below.

The little shepherd girl sleeps on a hill of wildflowers with her sheep close around her. She dreams she is up in the night sky dancing on the stars.

The Healer —
Part Two

TWO YEARS LATER—NORTH AFGHANISTAN— AFTER JACK ESCAPES FROM THE P.O.W. CAVE

From a distance we see Jack and the Wolf. The raven. A twisted tree. A cathedral of snow-covered mountains loom ahead, framed against the bluest blue sky. The sun pours itself over the horizon—a crucible of liquid gold. The rabbit in the full moon rising.

ANOTHER DAY

Jack walks on, the Wolf follows. He comes upon a dead man, almost frozen solid. Flies buzz noisily.

Jack pulls off the man's boots. He puts them on his own feet. He takes the Man's turban and gloves. He wraps the turban around his neck, puts the gloves on his frozen hands.

Outlaws

Jack has transformed; now he looks more like a nomadic Afghan tribesman than an American soldier.

NIGHT

Snow falls, Wolf and Jack huddle together for warmth.

DAY

Jack in his sheepskin coat, his boot prints in the snow trail endlessly behind him. Huge white mountains loom ahead.

A single rifle shot. Jack turns to see the Wolf wobble and fall, red blood colors white snow. Jack runs to his wolf friend. He sits in the snow. Holds the Wolf's head in his lap. The Wolf feebly licks Jack's hand. Blood stains Jack's sheepskin coat. He looks into the Wolf's eyes. Strokes his head.

The Wolf's heartbeat drums in Jack's ears. The Wolf's big eyes glass over. Jack buries his face in the Wolf's fur, he holds the Wolf's nose and breathes the last wild scent of life deep into his lungs. He screams a cry of anguish into the vast empty wasteland. It echoes off the mountains in the cold crystal air.

A Humvee skids to a stop in the snow. Milo and another Marine jump out with automatic weapons. Milo's barrel still smoking, pointed at Jack's head.

HUMVEE—DRIVING

The vehicle grinds over rough frozen terrain. Over snowy hills, over arid rocky desert plains.

Milo and the Marine ride silently in the front seat. Milo looks in the rearview at Jack in the back seat, talking to himself in Navajo language. His eyes wide and crazed. His long scraggly hair blows in the cold wind. Sheepskin coat smeared with the blood of a Wolf.

SECTOR 4—TEMPORARY NORTH AFGHAN OPS HEADQUARTERS—COMMANDING OFFICER'S TENT.

Floors made of loose sheets of plywood. Crates of rations, gear and weapons stacked in random piles.

Jack faces a serious-looking officer, Field Lieutenant Commander George Headly. "Your report says that you say you were captured and held as a prisoner of war." Jack silent.

Commander Headly: "Our intel however shows that there are not and never were any military prisoners of war taken in Operation Enduring Freedom… so you must be a deserter. You must be AWOL.

Jack, "These—all dead—were Prisoners of War." He rips off his chain, loaded with dog tags and slams it down on the table. Headly pushes the tags away into a trash can.

Headly: "Our report shows that you were with enemy insurgents when they shot down an Army Blackhawk."

Jack looks down, silent. Headley wears a head set. In the next room, Milo, red-faced yells into his headset, veins popping in his neck. "He's a goddamn traitor, he aided the goddamn enemy!"

Headly continues, "And you rendered medical assistance to enemy Taliban military personnel." Jack remains silent.

"Let me ask you one more question soldier. How do you respond to these charges...?"

Jack silent.

"I see. Well then, Reserve Corpsman Lieutenant Yahzee. I have no other option than to charge you with treason, desertion, and aiding the enemy. Punishable by life in military prison. You will be stripped of your rank and detained until your official court martial. Sergeant of The Watch, take this man out of my sight."

Jack and two armed guards leave the tent and climb into a Humvee. The Guards roll down the windows. One lights a cigarette.

On the other side of the tent complex, a suicide Afghan man with a crazed look on his face drives an ammo truck full of explosives. He closes his eyes. A crumpled photo of his dead family clipped to the visor. Rows of sticks of dynamite strapped to his body. He mashes the gas pedal. The big truck bumps over the cement barrier.

The wild-eyed Afghan plows it into the General's tent and presses the detonator button. The tent erupts in a huge fireball.

Inside the Humvee, Jack, handcuffed, rips open the door. The guard yells, "Stay in the vehicle! That's an order soldier! Stay in the vehicle."

Jack is gone. The door hangs open. Jack charges toward the burning tent like a berserk life-saving robot and disappears into the flames.

Jack tears through the fire. He traces his way back, finds Headley, still in his chair, unconscious. He throws him over his shoulder and runs back out through the fire. And rolls Headley in the dirt to put out his burning clothes.

Jack charges back in, his own clothes on fire. He sees Milo wandering around coughing, on fire, disoriented. Milo falls, overcome with smoke. Jack drags Milo out by his legs...

COMMERCIAL AIRLINES PLANE—TARMAC— NIGHT

Jack's hands are bandaged. The flight attendant announces "if you are traveling with a small child, first affix the oxygen mask over your own face before you assist the child.'

The 747 takes off, Jack looks out the window. They fly over a city lit up with sparkling lights.

Dog tags of the dead prisoners of war jingle in Jack's head.

Outlaws

In Jack's head, machine guns spit bullets. Jack imagines bombs going off on the American city below, etching city streets and buildings with fiery orange explosions.

The airplane descends for landing. It glides low over wide highways, the roofs of cars and trucks rush by below. The landing gear motors whir and the wheels CLUNK into their sockets.

ON THE RUNWAY

Jack sees through the window. The line of Afghans carry their possessions, trudge toward the caves that will be their glass tombs, leave their homes that have survived for decades of wars.

Beautiful Sahara, his love, dressed in black flowing robes walks slowly, gracefully. She floats over the runway beside Jack's window, her baby sucks milk from her breast. She turns her scarfed head to look into Jack's face. Their eyes lock for a brief eternity.

Her eyes show no remorse, no regret, no emotion. Then tears run down her cheeks as she fades and disappears with the others.

Tires screech on tarmac. The plane bounces. Jet engines roar, the brakes dig in and safe, familiar America comes into focus. Jack takes a ragged breath. No smile. No elation. No celebration.

Two MP Guards escort Jack to the arrival lobby, they

move through the crowd. Nobody waits for Jack at the gate. Nobody calls out his name. Nobody rushes to him. No sweet-smelling hair presses against his face. No warm flesh, no heartbeat at his chest. No tender tears of joy. No "Welcome to America soldier." Jack Yahzee has returned. Jack Yahzee is back home.

MILITARY BUILDING WASHINGTON DC

A room of darkly varnished wood. A long mahogany table stretches before Jack.

Seated at the table, half a dozen Senior Officers.

General Kruse speaks dryly, "Lieutenant Reserve Corpsman Jack Yahzee." He looks at Jack. Jack answers with his silence. Emotionless, he looks down through the varnished wood, to some distant place. No reply.

General Kruse pauses and continues, "Lieutenant Reserve Corpsman Jack Yahzee. This panel finds..." He shuffles papers. Looks at Jack trying to imagine what could have happened to turn a well-trained soldier into the vacant-eyed man who slumps before him with long, dirty hair, wearing a sheepskin vest smeared with dead blood. "This court marshal panel asserts... that... you were absent without leave, although you claim to have been held prisoner of war, a claim which we cannot corroborate. And that you administered medical aid to an enemy Taliban General. That you in fact administered life-saving medical assistance to a Taliban General. Although you claim to have been forced at gunpoint, another claim we cannot corroborate."

He pauses and looks at Jack. "You are hereby charged with two counts of treason, a charge which I must inform you is punishable by two consecutive life terms in military prison without parole." He looks at Jack. "Do you understand the charges?"

Jack makes no response. "Stand up Lieutenant." Jack stands. Two MP's step up to flank him.

An MP approaches and hands the General more papers. The General reads the newly arrived papers... "Furthermore, that also you then escaped from custody."

He looks at Jack scornfully, then reads more, "Against orders, no less, to remain in custody, is this correct? And you then willingly, contrary to direct orders did enter... an explosion... entered a burning tent... to save the life of one Commander Headly who had just charged you with treason, which bears a life sentence."

He tries to swallow the lump in his throat, looks up at Jack again. "And you then re-entered the burning tent, again, while you were...on fire bodily and your hands were handcuffed...to..." General Kruse wipes tears from his eye... he is choked up... clears his throat, "...to save the life of the officer who tracked you down and captured you...?"

He looks up at Jack, and reads some more murmuring... "just uncategorically remarkable..." He looks at Jack again, takes off his reading glasses. "I have never in all my career in the Navy... and as Commanding Officer of this Court Martial Tribunal..." Still looking at Jack "...witnessed such acts of uncommon bravery of this caliber!"

He wipes a tear from his eye, he is visibly moved... he takes his hat off, eyes never leaving Jack's eyes "Corpsman Jack Yahzee. It is clear to me that you have acted with outstanding and uncommon valor and selfless bravery."

The General looks at the other members of the tribunal, they all nod in agreement.

They all take off their hats. "All charges against you have been dismissed."

He pounds his gavel.

Jack's head slowly rises.

General Barten whispers to General Kruse. General Kruse nods to General Barten.

General Barten: "Lieutenant Yahzee, you are hereby officially commended to receive the Bronze Star and a Purple Heart for saving lives while injured and for exceptional bravery in battle and exemplary wartime service in combat."

All Officers rise to their feet and salute Jack.

Jack looks at the rows of medals hanging on the officers' chests. He hears machine gun fire, children scream,

Outlaws

bombs explode, dog tags jingle.

He turns and walks toward the door.

"I don't want your medal. Combat? I didn't never fight your stupid wasteful war."

He leaves the room and slams the heavy mahogany door.

The Healer—
Part Three

SKANKY ALBUQUERQUE BAR—NIGHT

Jack sits at a small table, pounds back Jack Black and cans of Bud Light. He looks like a badass biker. He wears torn dirty Levis. His hair long and stringy.

The hood of a blue sweatshirt over his head, his worn brown bloodstained sheepskin coat with the sleeves chopped off over that.

His head falls to the table. Dog tags jingle, machine guns rattle.

JACK'S HOUSE—MORNING

Jack looks real bad. He needs a lot more than strong coffee, a good breakfast and a hot shower.

A knock on the door.

He edges it open a crack. It's his old EMT partner Matt Black, "Hey, buddy. Heard you were back."

Jack doesn't invite him in. Door still cracked, "You alright, pal?"

Jack rubs his neck, "Yeah, fine."

"Yeah, well, hey, I talked to the boss. Said you can have your old job back whenever you're ready."

"I'll let you know, see you around." Jack closes the door.

KITCHEN

He pours himself a coffee.

When he turns around, his sister is at the kitchen table, watching him "Look, you really have to pull out of this. You think you're such a tough guy, that you don't need anybody, you go moping around all the time and... well, go see a doctor, Jack get some help, do whatever you have to do." Jack ignores her, "You have a really great little kid. Anna deserves to have a better father, a real father."

Angry voices scream in Jack's head and dog tags rattle, "Got to go." He opens the door and steps out.

Libby calls after him, "When are you going to stop running from yourself?"

BIKER BAR—NIGHT

Neon beer signs. Pool tables. Gnarly Bikers. Jack sits at a table by himself drinking beer.

The Bikers turn into the Dead Prisoners of War.

Jack looks through the window.

Moe, a heavy, tattooed biker roars up on a hog. His blonde babe Siouxie, on the back, wears overalls with not a whole lot underneath. Jack looks out the window at Siouxie, sees in her the girl he met and fell in love with, Sahara from Afghanistan. He stands.

Moe dismounts. Through the window Moe catches Jack looking at Siouxie and sees her smile at Jack.

He shouts at her and slaps her hard across the face. Her lip bleeds. Moe yells, "You stay here bitch!"

Moe storms into the bar and steams right up to Jack's table, "Saw you lookin'. You want her?"

Jack ignores him.

Moe yells, "What's your problem?"

Jack silent. Takes a sip of beer. Picks up a salt shaker.

Moe, "Come outside and we'll straighten this out."

Jack nods, leaves the bar walking behind Moe.

Moe wears a biker jacket. Big letters on his back announce, "DEVIL'S DISCIPLES."

Jack, following Moe, says, "What do you know about the devil?" Jack pours the rest of his bottle of beer on the back of the jacket and whacks Moe over the side of the head with the empty beer bottle.

Moe rubs his head, "You dumb suicidal motha'."

Moe hauls out a big switchblade. He presses the button

and the gleaming blade ejects. He swings at Jack.

Jack kicks the knife out of his hand. It skitters along the pavement.

Jack smashes Moe in the face, a salt shaker from the bar in his fist.

Moe stumbles and falls backward over the curb. Jack is on top of him.

A crowd of bikers gathers. They pull Jack away. Moe out cold.

Jack moves over to Moe's hog, gets on and says to Siouxie, "Get off."

"No. Take me with you."

They blast off, rpms red-lining. Car alarms **scream** as they roar past. Flames spit from the blue pipes.

Siouxie's fingers squeeze into Jack's chest. Her leg wraps around him. Her heels rub into his crotch.

MOTEL ROOM—NIGHT

Siouxie asleep on the bed fully clothed. Waits for Jack to come to her. But he never does.

Jack in a chair watches Siouxie. Sahara rises out of Siouxie's sleeping body. Sahara dressed in black, her head and face covered. She moves slowly up to him and removes her scarf. She shakes out her long beautiful raven hair and looks at Jack with big soulful glassy dark eyes. Her entire body throbbing for him.

He rises. Reaches for her.

To feel her in his arms one more time. His heart pounding. Aching for her. Echoing against the cheap wallpaper.

She vanishes.

Jack stands there in the dark room.

In the bathroom, Jack looks at himself in the mirror. His face is bloody. His hands and knuckles bleed. He pulls off his clothes.

In the shower, he leans against white tile. Steaming water cascades over him.

A Wolf howls.

Jack puts on his jeans, opens the door.

He walks outside.

Moe beside his hog, dried blood on his head.

Five raunchy bikers wearing Devil's Disciples jackets hover by their sleds, hold baseball bats and chains.

Siouxie looks out from the motel door. She screams.

The Manager looks through the curtains out the office windows, dials 911.

Moe, "Prepare to die scumbag."

Moe holds his hand up to his buddies stopping their advance.

"No, I'm gonna do this myself."

He swings a baseball bat repeatedly into his palm as he

moves toward Jack.

A passing police cruiser skids into the parking lot, all sirens and lights.

The cop calls back-up, pulls his shotgun off the rack, steps out of the cruiser, "Hold it right there."

He nods at Jack, "Hey Jack. When'd you get back?"

He saunters up to Moe with the confidence of a policeman holding a shotgun, "Lemme see you put down that bat nice and slow and put your hands nice and high against that nice wall."

Moe lowers the bat, walks to the wall, spits tobacco juice on the Cop's shoe.

"Rest of you, go on home. Now!"

The others get on their Harleys and rumble away.

The Cop cuffs Moe. And prods him into the back of his cruiser.

SUNRISE

Jack stands alone on the lawn of the motel in the dewy grass.

He lowers the motel American flag to half-mast.

STREETS—HARLEY—DRIVING

Jack, alone, blasts through a stop sign. The light turns red, he roars through it. Horns honk.

He stops at a green light, holds his hands over his ears.

But that makes the voices louder; the laughing and yelling continues.

Jack yells, "SHUT UP! SHUT UP!"

MORNING

Jack rides the Harley Chopper creeping at five miles per hour.

Cars, trucks, honk.

Jack rides faster and faster, passes semis. The broken white line whizzes by.

He skids off the interstate and screams along a desert two-lane.

A hand-written sign on a stick—an arrow points to the distant hills to:

HOPETOWN, NEW MEXICO

Jack hits the brakes.

The bike fish-tails, back tire smokes. Jack blows a u-turn and follows the arrow to HOPETOWN. Carves a trail of dust toward the ghost hills.

A crow flies overhead.

A Wolf watches from a hill.

Jack rides through the old mining ghost town.

He sees the people of Hopetown, Afghanistan walking the street—Bo, Qalzai, Stevens, the Guards, the women, the children beating on drum buckets and carrying stick rifles, Afghan men, old women, POWs bleeding, burned, wounded.

Sweet Sahara carrying her baby, the Wolf follows her.

Jack rides through town, looking at them.

When he wheels the bike round at the end of main street—they are all gone.

Jack gets off the bike and walks through the desert.

He stops over a plant, says a prayer and picks two peyote buds.

The Healer —
Part Four

WINDOW ROCK, NEW MEXICO

The giant gaping hole, big enough for a house to fall through, in the richly red-colored, tilting, ribbon-stratified rock-face, looms in front of him.

Jack walks in the tall dry golden grass under the most sacred of sacred places, Window Rock, the spiritual center of the Navajo Nation.

Around his neck, dog tags reappear. They shine, sparkle and jingle, translucent in the bright sunlight.

Jack hears the constant noise of The Dead he couldn't save chattering, and dog tags jingle in Jack's head.

Jack closes his eyes and sees a quick blur of men squirming and dying; children, women wounded; dying, limbless Marines; bombs exploding; machine guns rattling, spitting bullets; the dying screaming and begging him for help.

Jack holds his ears, but the noise only grows worse.

Jack yells, "STOP!"

A few tourists move in slow motion, separated from him by a stone wall.

Jack picks wild sage.

He lights the sage and offers the smoke up to Father Sky.

Then he offers the smoke down to Mother Earth.

Then to the Four Directions.

Jack and his Grandfather's voice together say a Navajo prayer.

Jack sprinkles corn pollen and lies down in the tall grass.

He disappears, private from their view, the noise in his head and jingle of dog tags fades.

Jack chews the peyote.

An Eagle soars searching for the bluest part of the sky.

Jack hears his grandfather, "When you find harmony. You too will then follow the Medicine Way, you are here to protect life. All life is sacred."

Sahara appears standing, beautiful, ethereal, dressed in black, her baby sucking at her breast, raven-black hair blowing in the wind.

Her love of life and her love for Jack encouraging him; a

sparkle in her haunting dark eyes. She whispers, "yes, yes, it is time."

Jack places his left hand inches above his heart.

He knows he must heal himself.

His arm and hand shakes—his grandfather, the Hand-trembler, Navajo healer.

Then his hand shakes violently.

Jack closes his eyes.

His face beads with sweat.

His right hand traces three Navajo symbols in the earth: The Purifying Sun. Harmony. The Healer.

Jack's entire body shakes violently.

He now stands, shaking.

His left hand inches from his heart, encased behind the bars in his chest, pounding against his rib cage to be free.

His entire body shaking now.

The noise, moanin', and jingling, continues.

Then the Ghosts of The Dead leave Jack's body. They are sucked upward through the giant hole in Window Rock as if swept away by the rush of a powerful transmordial solar wind.

The noise and dog tag jingling diminishes.

Dog tags one-by-one disappear.

Jack stands looking up at glorious sacred Window Rock.

Outlaws

At the sacred blue sky.

Only the sound of the wind in the tall grass and the vacuous, silent, ephemeral sucking sound of the giant hole of sacred Window Rock in his ears.

His arms are straight out, palms to the sun.

They tremble no more.

A soft wind blows his long black hair.

For the first time in a long, long time, there is a seraphic, peaceful look upon Jack's face.

The three Navajo symbols Jack drew in the dirt:

Purifying Sun. Harmony. The Healer—are now tattooed on Jack's chest.

Two Caves

Based on true stories

Radio announcer: "On All Things Considered this afternoon, this strange story comes to us from the foreign office of the AP Wire Service. It seems that a thirteen-year-old Syrian girl in a bold move, refuses to marry the man chosen by her family to be her husband. She is taken to a cave..."

A teenage girl is led into a cave by five clerics dressed in ceremonial robes.

They push her down to sit on a rock. They hold her roughly and tie her hands and feet. The five clerics form a circle around her and frown. They each spit on her. They count five steps from her. Each stands behind a pile of stones.

The men scold her and yell. She cringes at their harsh words.

Then they silently unroll small prayer rugs, kneel, place their foreheads on the rugs and pray. The girl pulls at the ropes that bind her hands and feet. When the prayers are made, one reads aloud from a book. He passes the weathered ancient book to the next man in the circle, who in his turn reads aloud. The last cleric to read places the book respectfully on a prayer rug. Each man rolls up his prayer rug except for the one with the book.

The leader looks down, not casting his eyes on the girl who cries and pleads with teary dark eyes. She knows that she will soon die. She will never smell a flower or stand beneath the blue sky and bright sun again. Her punishment is written. The girl looks at the stones. *Which will be the one that kills me? Please, please let it happen quickly.*

The leader picks up and hefts the largest stone—it is dark and sharp and heavy. Each of the other four men choose the largest stone, not looking into her eyes. The leader yells at the girl who cowers at his voice.

He raises the large sharp stone to his shoulders and reaches back to get a good hard throw. *This truly is Man's work, God's work,* his eyes say.

The girl wipes her tears with bound hands and now sits defiantly, head proud, no longer cowering from her assailants. *I am ready now to die.*

The leader slowly freezes. Eyes wide, He smells an unfamiliar odor, both wild and strong. He lowers the stone with a look of amazement. His open mouth reveals his rotted teeth.

A Lioness slowly enters the cave and with magnificent grace, looks into the eyes of each of the men as she walks in a fierce circle around the girl.

The men drop their stones and run from the cave.

The Lioness walks in a slow circle of protection around the girl until her friends come for her. Without a word, they untie her, surround her and escort her from the cave into the bright sunlight.

The Lioness lies down, tilts her huge head and growls softly.

Two Caves
Part Two

September four, eighteen hundred and eighty-six, Skeleton Canyon, Arizona.

My name is Goyaale. I am Mescalero Bedokone Chiricahua Apache. They call me Geronimo. I hide in the cave of my Grandfather's stories. Outside, General Miles and five thousand Seventh Cavalry hunt for me.

My horse, my brothers, my friends… all dead… killed by the Army long rifle. I lie in a puddle of my own blood. I look out at the mouth of the cave as the light goes dark… A Bear.

He lumbers ominously into the cave toward me, sniffing the air. The ground shakes with each step. Foam drips from his quivering lip. His teeth, his claws, long and sharp. He moves close to my face to smell me.

I feel his heat and smell decaying forest trees turning to earth. I look into the deep black lakes of his eyes and say to him:

"Mato, my brother, you know me, I am no better than you are. We both picked wild berries together when there was no other food. We both felt the cold in winter and the summer heat. I am your brother, Goyaale—I never hunted or hurt you. I kept the hunters away from your young. I know this is your home. If it is your wish, I will leave."

The Bear looks at me silently.

Outside in a noisy cloud of dust, a young soldier dismounts his tired horse. He is a dirty and frightened teenager wishing he had never left the family farm, wishing he never joined the Cavalry, and wishing he were not hunting this elusive, hard-to-kill damn Indian. He pulls an Army Sharps from his saddle. He leans into the edge of the mouth of the cave and sights along his rifle barrel, squinting into the darkness.

The Bear turns away from me, stands up on his back legs, spreads his huge arms, blocking the soldier's view of me and **roars** loudly, shaking the earth.

The young soldier falls backwards, picks himself up, rushes to his horse, mounts up and gallops away.

The Bear lies beside me, growls softly, his eyes guard the entrance.

High Seas

SAN FRANCISCO—RAPID TRANSIT TUNNEL 24C UNDER CONSTRUCTION

We peer into the hole in the side of a hill and cautiously track inside. The dark tunnel is sparsely lit by a string of naked light bulbs. A huge generator roars. Water drips randomly from the earthen tunnel roof. Two white spitting fireballs of a Lincoln Arc Welder illuminate two welders on ladders at work inside.

Welder Sam lifts off his face-guard and inspects his weld, takes out a chipping hammer and bangs off the slag. He grabs a wire brush from his leather apron and cleans up the bead. He hammers on the weld once more with his chipping hammer, looks up close and spits tobacco.

A noisy colony of nocturnal flying bats beat black veiny wings—screeching toward the light of day—anxious to be out of this creepy dank place. Suddenly the I-beam he was welding begins to distort. "Huh? What the...?" Sam mutters and spits tobacco again.

A LOUD CREAKING NOISE—THEN—CRASH!

As the entire tunnel structure gives way, a billion tons of life-snuffing rock crash down. We back-pedal, frantic for the exit, quickly passing the slowest bats as dust and stones barf out the end of the tunnel into the careless day.

TITLE CARD: TWO DAYS BEFORE—SAN FRANCISCO RAPID TRANSIT—CITY BUS DEPOT

Shiny new rectangular-shaped city buses parked in rows. City Bus Number Five One Seven, out of place, round-cornered, old style, splattered with graffiti, squats by its lonely self on the cement slab; a black puddle of oil and diesel spreads under the open engine compartment.

A man's head, shoulders and arms are inside the beast, working on the archaic diesel. The man flips down his welder's helmet, lights up an acetylene torch and welds something inside. He pulls his head and arms out, quickly reaches back in to beat out a small fire with a glove and pops off the torch. He wipes a wrench with a red rag, white steam comes from his breath as he whistles the blues.

This is Daren, 40s. He has an honest face, smudged with grease, and a twinkle in his eye. Henry, the old black yard mechanic in stained overalls walks by carrying a tool box. "Hey Daren, still trying to save the world?"

"No, Henry, just trying to save this old bus."

"What fo'?"

"Can't just throw it away. This is the best bus on the lot."

"Don't try to stop the gears of progress son. It'll grind you up."

Daren clomps around the bus, waving his hands over it as if blessing the ancient contraption and jumps for the driver's seat. He holds down the glow plug toggle for ten heartbeats and turns the key. The diesel growls and coughs black smoke.

"Come on… baby. Come on… baby."

The engine starts, cycles and evens out to a smooth clatter.

Nearby, City Bus Driver Michael mounts a newer bus, starts it up, pulls alongside the one Daren's working on, opens the window and leans out.

"Hey Daren, why don't you let that one go where the dinosaurs went?"

"This one's made in America, not in China like yours; there's nothing wrong with this one."

"Yeah right, that's why you're always fixing it. You should tow it to the scrap yard with the new tow truck."

"No way, it's got a heart and soul and a two-stroke GM six-seventy-one diesel; best diesel America ever made."

"Comin' to the staff party tomorrow?"

"Thought I'd go over see Susan."

"Dude you *really* need to find a new girl and a new pet project. Check out the beach after work, maybe meet up at secret rock and carve some waves..."

"Yeah sounds cool."

Michael smiles and drives away. Daren eases the lid of the old bus closed and steps out of his overalls, underneath, a white shirt and Levis. He heads toward the B.A.R.T. office.

Just by his look, you'd trust this guy to do the right thing.

Inside B.A.R.T. Headquarters. Daren walks past Sheila, the perky receptionist.

"Hi, Daren. Coming to the staff party Saturday night?"

"Hey, Sheila, maybe."

Daren enters a private office with CITY ENGINEER painted on the door in black with gold leaf. Through the glass windows we watch the redheaded City Engineer un-roll a set of blueprints. They both lean over the plans. Daren points at something. A heated discussion follows.

OCEAN BEACH—SUNSET

Daren and Michael surf, carving away the stress of the day. The Golden Gate Bridge towers behind them.

CITY MARINA LATER

Daren slides his surfboard on deck, takes off his shoes and climbs onboard his sailboat, *Pirate*. Daren sighs, "Sweet home at last."

He ducks below and snaps on a cabin light. Through the portholes we catch cozy glimpses of the varnished teak, the honey-colored interior of the sailboat, Daren cracks open a bottle of beer.

DAREN'S PICKUP TRUCK—EARLY NEXT MORNING

CONVENIENCE STORE PARKING LOT

In the middle of the truck's door, a big round sticker: B.A.R.T. • SAN FRANCISCO • BAY AREA RAPID TRANSIT. And below that: EXTENSION PROJECT SUPERVISOR.

Daren sits behind the wheel of the new black diesel pickup—windows up, heater humming, dome lights—he leafs through an engineering book. He bites at the eraser end of the pencil, makes notes and draws construction diagrams, finishes the last of his sandwich and gulps a drink of steaming hot coffee.

Then in his notebook, beside the engineering diagrams, he draws: a sailboat sailing past an island with one palm tree and drives off.

Daren stops the truck at Tunnel 24 B. John, a bulldog of a construction worker, hard hat, overalls, ambles up to Daren's window, "Yo, Daren, howzit?"

"Fine, John, how's this side of the planet?" Daren snaps open a cold can of Coke and hands it to John who takes a big gulp as he unrolls a set of blueprints, "This can't be right, can it boss?" John points at something on the blueprint.

"It's not, should be twenty-seven feet. Spacing's wrong. Had a meeting about that with the Engineer yesterday."

John: "Redheaded corner-cutting asshole City Engineer must of been in a hurry to play free golf on Wednesday."

"Yeah, you're right. How's your boy's knee, John"?

"Oh, it's healing slow. Want to come over watch football Sunday?"

"Got a ton of stuff to do on the boat. Peace bro."

Daren starts up the truck and drives away.

TUNNEL TWENTY-FOUR C—LATER

Daren shines his flashlight at a welded overhead beam in the ill-fated underground tunnel. Sam shuts down his welder box and moves over to Daren's truck. Daren hands him a cold can of soda and a pack of Copenhagen chewing tobacco, says, "Should have been a one-inch load-bearing web gusset, not five eighths, Sam."

"Okay boss, I'll cut 'em off and bead up new ones."

Daren shines his flashlight at the other I-beams. "One at a time... wait a second, these are all too light." He spreads out the blueprints, "I-beam spacing's way off in this section too." Daren makes some notes. "Something's screwy. City engineer's been screwing up, he's gonna to have to redraw this entire tunnel. Everything's way too under-sized." He makes more notes. "Meantime, go ahead, prefab up a stack of one-inch gussets. And set up intermediary bridge I-beams every other set—there," Daren points, "There—and there."

"Okay boss."

ANOTHER CONSTRUCTION SITE

A truck stacked with steel plate pulls up beside Daren's truck. "You want me to sign for this?"

Driver checks his invoices, "Looks like you already did. After you faxed and changed the order."

"Let's see that." Daren examines the signature on the clipboard, "That's not my signature!"

LATER

Daren drives up in his nice old '60s pickup truck, a surfboard on the rack. He parks and goes into a Victorian style apartment building. Daren knocks on the door. He knocks again. "Susan, open up baby, it's me."

The double chained door creaks open six inches.

Susan, with just-got-out-of-bed-hair, wearing an extra-large football shirt, looks out at Daren. "Go away Daren. Just go away. It's over." She closes the door. Daren stands for a moment, long enough to hear inside Susan's apartment.

The redheaded City Engineer holding a golf club stands

behind Susan, smoking a cigar. "Who the fuck was that?"

Susan moves away from the door. "Nobody."

Daren hears that, slams his fist into the wall and slinks down the hallway.

STAFF PARTY—SATURDAY NIGHT

Loud recorded blues music pours its guts out into the smoky living room. People drink, dance, make out, nod out, and pass out. Daren, slightly out of it himself and out of place, moves down the crowded hallway.

Sheila, the perky B.A.R.T. secretary, pressed against the wall, kissing some guy. Daren squeezes past them on his way to the kitchen. "Hey Sheila."

She half-opens her eyes, notices Daren, pulls her mouth off her date's face. "Oh, hi Daren, you made it. Yay!"

Above the din someone somewhere else yells, "Why do we do it?... Because we're BART!" A whole roomful of drunken party-goers yell, "Because we're B.A.R.T. Yeah!"

KITCHEN

Daren snags a beer from the fridge, cracks it, takes a swig. He draws a sailboat sailing past a palm tree island in the condensation on the window.

A hand passes him a joint. His buddy Michael, "Ere bro," he coughs.

"No thanks, that's okay. I'll stick with beer."

Michael sees the sailboat drawing on the window, "Still

dreaming about sailing?"

"Yeah dreaming, can't afford to sail anywhere right now."

Michael offers the joint to Daren again. "Dude, take a hit, it's Saturday night, we don't work tomorrow, you're only alive once, 'ere."

Daren shakes his head "no" again.

"How's Susan?"

In Daren's memory:

Susan slams the door. Daren hears, "Who the fuck was that?" and Susan says, "Nobody."

Another ex-girlfriend punches Daren in the face, pushes him backward down the stairs with her cowboy boot and slams the door.

Another ex-girlfriend throws a bouquet of flowers at him and slams a door in his face.

And yet another tattooed ex-girlfriend drives a cement truck over Daren's motorcycle.

Michael asks again, "You see Susan?"

Michael shoves the joint at Daren again. "Here, you look like you need this."

"No, I don't want to talk about her and I don't want any of that!"

Daren takes a big swig of beer and swallows hard, trying to drown the suck out of his memory of Susan. He throws the empty bottle into the garbage can and opens another.

CITY MARINA, LATER

Daren pulls into a parking space. He goes down the springy gangway, along the floating dock. An old man stares at a sailboat in the slip across from *Pirate*, then walks down the dock toward Daren: "Hey Daren."

The man stops Daren on the dock: "Don't you make the mistake I did, got too busy making money to enjoy my boat, then one day I got too old. Sail that boat son, until there's no more ocean left to sail." The man smiles meekly and is gone.

Daren approaches his sailboat. He presses his forehead against the hull, "You want to spread your wings, don't you *Pirate*?"

He takes off his boots, hops onboard in his socks and disappears below.

PIRATE—SUNDAY MORNING

Daren, wearing pajama bottoms, rescues a frosty beer from the icebox, snaps it open and takes a big swig. He pulls out another drawing of a sailboat and an island and places it on a stack with the other sailboat drawings.

Daren's phone rings. He looks at the caller ID: B.A.R.T. OFFICE. Sheila, the secretary, is on the other end. She looks around nervously, making sure nobody's listening.

"Daren, hey, it's Sheila, um..."

"Oh, hi Sheila, what's up? You wanna go out sometime?"

Sheila, nervous, "Stop it Daren, listen to me. There was an accident. Tunnel Twenty-four C collapsed, two welders...are, well...they're dead."

"Damn! Was Sam in there?"

"Yeah, Sam and Arturo didn't get out."

She hangs up.

"Dammit."

His phone rings again.

Phone ID: B.A.R.T. GENERAL MANAGER. "Hello Daren, Jim Fox over at BART."

"Hi Jim, what's up?"

"Hear about the accident?"

"Just found out. All the steel structure in the city engineer's plans were way under-sized. And someone's been forging my signature, signing for material deliveries."

"That's not what the city engineer said. Police detectives were here already asking questions. They want to talk to you Daren. Have to let you go. Come in Monday. Clean out your desk. Sorry." Jim hangs up.

Daren looks at his phone, hangs up and puts down his beer, "Damn!"

His phone rings again, Daren picks up, "What?"

Sheila: "I heard the City Engineer tell the cops that you re-drew the plans, sold the heavier steel and bought lighter stuff and put the difference in your pocket. Be careful Daren."

Outlaws

The line goes dead.

Daren's phone rings again.

"Yeah?"

Michael on the other end: "Hey Daren, city engineer set you up. You're going down buddy."

"How bad?"

"Real bad."

"What should I do? What would you do?"

"I'd get in that boat of yours and disappear till this blows over."

"Yeah, you're right, I need some time to figure this out."

"Let me know if I can help. Stay easy dude." Michael hangs up.

Daren disconnects the electrical cord and says to his boat, "Now we're unplugged. Can't let them take us down. I won't go to prison for something I didn't do. Can't lose you now. One more payment and you're mine, free and clear."

He starts the diesel. Unties his boat. And motors *Pirate* out of the slip. He leans, reaches over the side and places his hand on the hull, as if *Pirate* were a big race horse and he were the jockey, "I know you're ready."

Pirate motors, quietly sneaking out of the marina.

PIRATE'S DOCK—LATER

Two uniformed Police arrive on the dock. *Pirate's* gone. The Old Man on the sailboat across from Daren's sees the Police at *Pirate's* empty slip and smiles. One Cop pulls out a photo of *Pirate* and Daren. Shows it to the Old Man who just shakes his head "no." Cop looks at his watch and records the time in his notebook.

FUEL DOCK—NIGHT

Daren ties *Pirate* up to a deserted fuel dock. He finds a hose and fills his water tank. He looks at one of the turn-buckles and follows it all the way to the top of the mast, then he says to *Pirate*, "We're going sailing, someplace they can't get us."

The water overfills, Daren turns off the hose. He unties *Pirate* and is underway.

SAN FRANCISCO BAY

Daren raises the sails, "Spread your wings lady..." *Pirate* catches a breeze, heels and sails. "YES!"

PACIFIC OCEAN—NIGHT

Daren sails under the mighty Golden Gate Bridge. He looks up at the cement, steel girders, cables and the hum and clatter of traffic above.

His sailboat seems very tiny in the vast ocean as it rises to the big lumpy groundswell. Daren eases the sails. He swings the wheel to port—heading south toward Mexico.

SAN FRANCISCO COAST GUARD DOCK—NIGHT

A Coast Guard Cutter speeds underway—blue light flashing and siren wailing.

RICHARDSON'S BAY, SAUSALITO—NIGHT

Coast Guard Cutter looks for *Pirate*, shines its spotlight on the transoms of sailboats at anchor.

PACIFIC OCEAN—NIGHT

Daren pulls down his radar reflector, tosses it below, sails into a fog bank and disappears.

OCEAN—DAY

Pirate sails through the fog. A faint ghost of a shape in front of them. A huge freighter crosses *Pirate's* path; *Pirate*, small, fragile and vulnerable. The freighter blows its horn. *Pirate* rolls in the freighter's bow wake.

OCEAN—ANOTHER DAY

Pirate plows through the waves. Broad reach, all sails set. Spray and flying fish. Daren asleep at the wheel.

ANOTHER DAY

Pirate sailing. Daren reels in a dorado.

HARBOR

TITLE CARD: CATALINA ISLAND

Pirate at anchor in Cat Harbor. Daren at the transom finishes changing the name of his boat to *Outlaw*.

Daren sleeps on deck in a hammock.

A marine patrol boat slowly motors by, checking the name on the transom of Daren's sailboat.

PACIFIC OCEAN—NIGHT—SAILING

The Big Dipper points at the North Star, shimmering low off *Outlaw's* stern.

Daren inhales a big breath of the dark starry night and smiles.

PACIFIC OCEAN—DAY—SAILING

Daren deep asleep, draped over the wheel.

Fishing rod bends almost in half.

A tiny bell attached to the end of the pole rings—ding, ding, ding, ding, ding. Daren wakes, grabs the fishing rod out of the holder and cranks like crazy on the reel.

PACIFIC OCEAN—EVENING—SAILING

Daren flips over a nice chunk of fish barbecuing on the grill in his cockpit.

OCEAN—DAY—SQUALL

Daren wears a safety harness snapped to the boat. There's zero visibility with hard-driving horizontal rain. Daren grits his teeth.

He wrestles with the flogging sail, he yanks down the jib. Windblown waves sledgehammer against *Outlaw's* hull.

Outlaws

OCEAN—DAY

A perfect sailing day. *Outlaw's* sails are full. They pull her with graceful majesty over the waves.

HARBOR—DAY

TITLE CARD: ACAPULCO MEXICO

Outlaw sails into the harbor. Big ostentatious sportfish boats zoom past. Typical fishing tournament stuff: big turbo diesels roar, kicking up wake, spray and foam—shiny fiberglass and chrome—scantily-clad trophy women sun on deck—gold-plated oversized electric fishing reels glint—custom-made fighting chairs—flags announce the boats have caught tournament-size fish.

Outlaw crashes and rolls in their wake, sails into the anchorage.

Daren lowers mainsail. He drops anchor, pays out chain. And backs the jib hard to set it. He pulls down the jib and surveys the anchorage, he whispers, "Welcome to Mexico, *Outlaw*." He dives overboard wearing mask and fins to make sure the anchor is secure. Daren swims back to *Outlaw* for his surfboard and a ziplock bag containing his wallet and a dry shirt, and paddles ashore.

ACAPULCO ALLEY—SAME DAY

Paper, soup cans, bottles, garbage cans. Scruffy dogs lick food wrappers, flies buzz.

Marlene, late twenties, exotic beauty without makeup, bronze skin and sparkling deep dark eyes, black hair with curls, sits behind a Taqueria, (small cafe), on a curb. Ten little street kids—orphans, dirty, barefoot, clothes torn, sores, one little girl has one leg and crutches, gather in a circle around Marlene. She musses their hair and tickles and pokes at them in a big-sisterly way.

Marlene presses a finger to her lips, "Shhh! We are going to practice speaking Gringo today." The children boo and sigh and roll their eyes. She begins, "Once there was a little girl. Just like you." She gently pokes the little girl with one leg in the stomach, the girl giggles. "She had no family and she lived alone in the street."

"Didn't she have no friends?"

"Well, maybe a few."

One little kid, "Me."

Another, "Me."

Another"Me too."

The kids giggle.

Marlene continues, "One day, the Queen of Mexico comes to town in a golden carriage pulled by seven big white horses."

The kids all listen wide-eyed.

"And as she looks out her window at the flying unicorn that always accompanied the royal coach, her purse tumbles out onto the street."

Little boy yells, "Is it filled with gold coins and cookies?"

Marlene answers, "Yes. And one of the little street boys grabs the purse and starts to run away with it." The little boys grin.

"But the little girl with one leg trips the running boy with her cane, pulls the purse away and hands it back to the Queen."

The little girls smile.

"Then the Queen steps out into the muddy street. Her maids, aghast, hold up her long white gown so it doesn't go in the muck."

"What's aghast?"

"Surprised. The Queen bends down and looks at the little girl with one leg's pretty face, she smiles and takes her by her hand.

"And brings her back to the coach with her. The Queen takes off her own muddy shoes and gets a new pair." Marlene holds her nose and pretends she is dropping invisible muddy shoes in a bag."

The kids giggle.

"And the little girl gets her dirty little foot wiped off with a warm wet towel and gets her very own fancy shoe."

The little street kids look down at their bare dirty feet. "Yay!" They clap and smile.

"The Queen of Mexico couldn't have no childrens of her own so she adopts the little one-leg street girl and the Queen's carpenter and blacksmith together made the little girl the most beautiful new leg in the world—she can skip and dance again—and they live in the big castle happily after ever."

The children clap their hands and yell "YAY!" One little street orphan girl wipes a tear from her eye, the story made her sad.

Meanwhile the back door of the Taqueria opens and the Cook steps out, "Vamoose." He yells.

A little girl answers, "But we are hungry and we thought you might have some broken food that you cannot sell."

"Go away or I call the policía!" the Cook growls. He slams the door.

Marlene and the children stand. The door opens again. The Cook brings out a stack of tortillas on a napkin, some broken or with missing edges. He places them on the step. "Take this and go!"

Marlene picks up the tortillas and hands one to each child.

ACAPULCO—STREETS

Marlene and the children move through the backstreets. A dinged-up black and white Volkswagen Beetle with POLICÍA written on the door rattles by slowly, the

Outlaws

Policeman watches them, making Marlene and the Children nervous.

MARINA PARKING LOT

Now Marlene and the street kids gather behind the chain-link marina fence, looking through it at a dumpster full of big blue marlin fish on the other side. An armed Soldier stands with a rifle beside the dumpster guarding the dead fish from thieves.

In the background Daren paddles his surfboard up to the dock. His sailboat rolls at her anchor behind him.

A little street urchin: "Look at all the fishes."

Little girl: "That could feed a hundred poor peoples."

One boy makes a small paper airplane and sends it looping through the fence toward the Soldier who swats it out of the air, stomps it with his army boot and frowns.

The girl with one leg taps her cane on the fence while another little girl holds her hand. The other children bang sticks and stones against the chain-link fence.

Kids chant, "Fishes! Fishes! Give us fishes!"

Daren, now wearing a Hawaiian shirt and board-shorts, carries his surfboard. He walks along a dock full of expensive yachts, mostly big American tournament sportfish boats. He climbs up the ramp to the land.

Once-magnificent, big, dead Blue Marlin are tagged and loaded onto dock carts. And taken to a booth where they are weighed, photographed and entered in a ledger.

Daren watches as the huge fish are then loaded back into dock carts.

He follows. The dead fish are wheeled around back into the parking lot. Two workers toss them into the dumpster and go back for another load. The Soldier stands by, holds a rifle and frowns.

Marlene and the kids wiggle through the gate and approach the dumpster.

One little boy: "Mister Soldier, please give us a fish, we are hungry."

Soldier grunts, "No. Go away. They are not for you, they belong to the rich gringos."

The Soldier points his rifle at Marlene and the approaching Children, "Stay back!"

Daren watches all this as he walks by with his surfboard. He passes in front of the Soldier. The Soldier lowers his rifle to let Daren pass. Daren swings his surfboard smack into the Soldier's chest and pushes him into the water.

Marlene and the children watch in surprise. They run up to the dumpster. Two kids climb in and try to pick up a big marlin by the head and tail, but it's too heavy.

Four more kids jump in and lift and push the fish up and over to the edge of the dumpster.

Four kids below stand with their hands out ready to catch

the big fish. Over goes the marlin. The kids get knocked down. They wiggle out from underneath it and get back on their feet.

They try to pick up the fish but it is too heavy to carry. One of the kids in the dumpster tosses down a piece of discarded rope. They fasten the rope around the fish's tail and half-drag, half-carry the fish back to the fence and squeeze it through the gate.

Marlene looks back at Daren and says to the kids, "That is the bravest Gringo I have ever saw."

Daren watches until they are safe. The Soldier, still flapping around in the water, tries to pull himself out but falls back in. Daren hides his surfboard in the bushes and walks away.

BAR—NIGHT

Daren sits alone and drinks a beer. Two empty bottles at his table.

ALLEY—NIGHT

A big fire burns in a steel drum. Lots of fish grill on top. A scruffy Mariachi Band plays a soulful Mexican folksong. A large group of street kids and other homeless enjoy the feast.

BAR—NIGHT—LATER

Daren finishes his cerveza. Now there are four empty bottles on his table. He opens his wallet, peels out a few dollar bills, lays them down and looks into his empty wallet.

Turns it upside down and shakes it. A B.A.R.T. token falls out. Daren picks up the coin and looks at it. *He sees Sam and Arturo on their ladders welding as the tunnel collapses.*

He closes his eyes to shut it out. But the vision of his friends being crushed to death in the tunnel becomes stronger with each beat of his heart. He puts his head down on the table and lifts it up as a Police Car roars down the street blasting its siren. Daren goes to the door. He stands in the doorway and watches.

A block away, the cop car skids to a stop. Two Cops and the Dumpster Soldier jump out. The Soldier points at Marlene who walks by herself on the sidewalk.

Soldier: "That's her." They charge after her. Marlene runs like a racehorse.

Later, Marlene hides behind a tree. She watches as Daren paddles out to *Outlaw*, climbs on board, pulls up his surfboard and goes below.

A police car drives by, aiming a searchlight at the trees, looking for Marlene.

OUTLAW—LATER

Daren in his bunk, closes his eyes. He hears scratching on the hull. He sits up, hitting his head, pulls on his pants and jumps up on deck.

Marlene, dripping, climbs up the transom swim-step, "Mister, the police, they are looking for me because of you. Can I hide here?"

"No. I got enough trouble without yours."

"But I have no place to go. If they find me... they will arrest me... and rape me... please, mister."

"Well you can't stay here."

"Maybe I was wrong about you, I tol' the orphans you were brave..."

Making herself at home, Marlene picks up the deck shower hose, "You mind?" Daren nods his head okay. She hoses herself off quickly and wipes her face and hair on a towel. Her t-shirt clings to her wet body, "But, they also look for you too, they will arrest and rape you too. And since you have to leave anyway, you might as well take me with you."

"No."

"We should sail to Zihuatenejo, I have a uncle there, Bictor, a farmer. We can work on his finca, he will pay us. It is only fifty miles from here."

"No. Absolutely not."

Marlene's t-shirt now almost transparent, "Please?"

Police cars shine spotlights on the boats in the anchorage. Daren grabs Marlene's hand and pulls her down to hide behind the cabin. A searchlight sweeps across *Outlaw's* deck.

Outlaw's sails go up in darkness.

OCEAN—DAY

Outlaw sailing, rising, gleaming to the Pacific swell. Sun-white sails full and pulling. Marlene looks around, she is overwhelmed by the sailing experience, "Wow! I never been sailing before."

"What were you doing with those kids back there?"

"It is kinda like flying, like when you are flying in your dreams. What is your name?"

"None of your business."

"That's so not nice. You know you could have more friends if you were nicer."

"I have lots of friends."

Marlene looks around, "Oh yeah? Where are they, that why you are sailing alone?"

Flying fish burst from the inky blue Pacific. White foamy waves hiss at the bow.

HARBOR—DAY

TITLE CARD: ZIHUATENEJO

Outlaw swings to her anchor.

"Before we go, I should tell you..."

"What?"

"Uncle Bictor is sick, he's soon gonna die."

"What's he got?"

"Heart problems."

"Too bad."

"High blood pressure, very high, glaucoma, chronic back ache, Lupus, insomnia..."

"That it?"

"No. Cancer, depression, nausea, loss of appetite, acute arthritis."

Daren puzzled, turns to look at Marlene.

UNCLE BICTOR'S FINCA—DAY

Uncle Bictor, a wise and kindly-looking old Mexican man, sun-baked, wrinkled, long white hair, stands with Marlene and Daren in a mountain field of huge budding healthy flowering marijuana plants.

Daren whispers to Marlene, "Your Uncle Bictor is a marijuana farmer? I don't remember you mentioning this little detail in Acapulco."

Six whistling Mexican laborers use machetes to dig around the roots of large cannabis plants.

Bictor smiles, "This is the perfect time to harvest. The moon is growing. The resins are high. This right now is the correct time, before the rains."

Marlene, "OK, we know this Uncle, the perfect time, we know."

She turns to Daren, "Just so you know, everyone on this mountain grows marijuana even the Chief of Police. Potatoes, corn don't grow here good. Neither do tomatoes. My Uncle Bictor grows the very best totally organic crop in all of Mexico."

Bictor places a machete in Daren's hand, "You must be careful not to cut the big root or the plant will bleed out its resin." He digs around the plant. "Like this."

A bird chirps. Suddenly, nearby machine-gun fire splatters the bucolic tranquility. Birds screech and rise into startled flight. Mexican Laborers drop their machetes and run away yelling, "Ay caramba!"

Daren, "And that would be?"

Bictor, "Oh that. That is nothing."

"Nothing?"

"My neighbor, the Chief of Police, he is a little irritated."

"Irritated? Something I should know?"

"Oh it is really nothing. He is a bit angry that I have not paid *la mordida*. But I have no money to pay him. Maybe after we sell the crop."

"Whoa! Slow down, did you say *we* sell the crops?"

Bictor watches the last laborer run away. "Now it is up to us three to harvest the entire crops. I will pay a hundred American dollars a day each, our work will be finished in four days. Then the plants, they will be hanging in the barn to dry like this" To demonstrate Uncle Bictor stands on his head with his tongue hanging out the side of his mouth.

MARIJUANA FIELD—NEXT DAY

Heat ripples above the healthy green plants that seem to extend into infinite space. More gunfire. Only about a quarter of the field is picked. Daren glances at sweaty Bictor working hard, he says to Marlene, "Uncle Bictor doesn't work like a man dying of cancer, chronic back pain and a bad heart."

Marlene swings her machete. "He believes in the medicinal power in his plants."

Daren works hard, carefully frees the root of a huge plant. He pulls off his t-shirt, sweat covers his body. Marlene labors nearby, catches a quick glimpse of Daren's muscular torso, and continues to work. She looks at Daren again.

Bictor, several yards ahead, drenched in sweat, pulls off his shirt too—not a pretty sight.

Daren yanks on a big plant with both hands. He turns the plant upside down, sticks out his tongue like Bictor had done. And carries it to a wooden wagon hitched up to Manuelito, the grumpy old mule. Manuelito bites the back of Daren's leg as he walks by.

"Hey! Watch that!"

Bictor also carries a big plant to the wagon. "What is it?"

"The donkey bit me."

"That is too bad señor Daren."

"Why?"

"Because all the donkeys in this part of Mexico have rabies."

Daren looks at Manuelito, the cranky animal is foaming at the mouth. "Nice."

Daren climbs on board and ties the plant upside-down to a wooden rack where other freshly-picked plants hang. Daren catches an innocent glimpse of Marlene, bronze, glistening with sweat and endorphins. He does a double-take while jumping down from the wagon as if noticing her graceful natural beauty for the very first time.

MARIJUANA FIELD—NEXT DAY

The crop is half-picked. More machine gun fire. Daren Marlene and Bictor ignore it, laboring away.

MARIJUANA FIELD—NEXT EVENING

Only a quarter of the field remains. Exhausted, Marlene climbs up and sits beside Bictor on the wagon full of hanging plants. Worn out, Daren trudges, holds Manuelito's reins, he hauls himself toward the barn, drags his machete behind him. The mule brays loudly protesting the heavy load. Daren turns to cop a quick look at Marlene who sighs in exhaustion, high-fives Bictor and laughs.

BARN—EVENING

Bictor and Daren roll open the barn door.

Bictor: "You know, there is too much stress in the world. The war in Iraq, Afghanistan, Syria, the economy, crazy hombres with guns, forest fires, hurricanes, your loco idiot president, people losing their jobs, their homes."

In almost every space, big-budded plants hang upside-down to dry.

"So why do I grow this crop you might ask? Because marijuana is the medicine for the people, a good medicine and it relieves pain and stress. Today it is stress that makes peoples sick." Marlene hears this and smiles. She cuts the plants down from the rack on the wagon and hands them to Bictor and Daren. They carry them into the barn, climb ladders and hang the plants from rafters to dry. Big noisy fans move the heavy resin-ladened air around the barn to speed drying. Daren returns to the wagon for another plant. He sees smoke and a red glow rising from the field in the distance.

BURNING FIELD—EVENING

The Chief of Police, laughing, drives his pickup swerving in the dusty dirt road away from the flames in Bictor's field, empty containers of gasoline rattle around in the bed. EL JEFE DE POLICÍA (CHIEF OF POLICE) the sign on the driver's door.

BARN—EVENING

Daren yells, "Bictor! Hey Bictor, look!"

Bictor rushes out and looks where Daren is pointing.

Bictor: "It does not matter now."

"But all those plants, we can save some of them."

"There is no more room in the barn. Let him think he is hurting us. In this business it is important not to be greedy." He shakes Daren's hand, "Thank you Mister Daren, you are a Gringo who works like three Mexicans." Then to Marlene, "And you... thank you my beautiful niece who works like a man but looks like a flower." He kisses her on the forehead. He then counts out American dollars and pays them. "Now we have just to find a way to take this to market, oh, and we have to find a market."

DONKEY STABLE—NIGHT

Daren and Marlene both sleep in separate donkey stalls on beds of hay. Manuelito the mule snores, still foaming at the mouth in Daren's crowded stall beside him.

"Pssst. Hey Marlene. What did Bictor mean, we have to find a way to take that stuff to market?"

"Oh. This is his first time doing this. He used to grow hay."

"But you said he's the best grower in Mexico"

"He is."

"Okay. And about finding a market?"

"He's kinda winging it if you know what I mean?"

"Uh huh. Okay then, good night."

"Good night. If you want, you can..." Daren snores. "Oh,

nevermind." Daren continues to snore. Marlene closes her eyes, hugs herself and drifts off to sleep.

BICTOR'S HOUSE—NEXT MORNING

Marlene knocks on the door and it creaks open. "Hey uncle, want us to make coffee?" Marlene and Daren enter. "Hey uncle. You still…" They walk into the living room. Uncle Bictor sits back in his easy chair. With a bullet hole dead center forehead. "Asleep?" She stands there, her hand over her mouth in shock. "Oh my!" And then runs to him. She falls to his knees and cries her eyes out.

Daren runs to the barn. He rolls open the big doors. Inside, half the plants are gone. Tire tracks lead off toward the Chief of Police's house.

Marlene, now by his side, still teary. Diagonally over her t-shirt she wears a wide brown leather belt stuffed with shotgun cartridges in each slot, like Pancho Villa.

Daren looks at Marlene. "Now what do we do?"

She puts her arm around Daren and her hand on his shoulder. "Hey Daren. I was thinking, we can fit this crops into your boat." She's now pointing her sawed-off, double-barreled, twelve-gauge shotgun casually at Daren's crotch.

High Seas
Part Two

BICTOR'S FARM HOUSE—SUNSET

Daren shovels the last bit of dirt on the grave.

Marlene writes "Uncle Bictor" on the little wooden cross, places a single marijuana leaf on the mound of earth, and wipes tears from her eyes.

BARN—NIGHT

Marlene: "These plants needs three more days to dry," still casually pointing the shotgun at Daren's crotch. "Then a day to pack and load, then we sail to California."

"You don't understand. I can't go back there."

Marlene pumps a cartridge into the firing chamber.

Daren"Where were you planning to get rid of this in California?"

"You said yourself you had a lot of friends. The Jefe took what he thought Uncle Bictor owes him, but he still could come back for more, he drinks lots of tequila and is a greedy man."

LATER

Daren guards the barn, asleep, snoring, leans against the barn door, a machete in his hand.

BARN—ANOTHER NIGHT

Marlene—awake—sits, leans against the barn door looks up at the moon and stars with the shotgun in her lap.

BARN—ANOTHER NIGHT

Daren—awake—sitting in the dirt, his back against the barn door, finishes a bottle of beer, talks to Manuelito who munches on some straw beside him.

"Sure I'm attracted to her."

Manuelito stops munching to look at Daren suspiciously.

Marlene lies in a bed of hay on the other side of the door. Hearing Daren say this, she opens one eye…

"Sure, I'd like to… you know… Geez, who wouldn't? She's beautiful."

On the other side of the barn door smiling she wags her finger from side to side, scoldingly.

"But there's something you should know..." Manuelito turns his head questioningly as he studies Daren.

Outside, Marlene gets up on her elbows and puts her ear

closer to the door.

Daren opens another beer. "I'm no good for her. I'm no good at relationship. I don't even have a dog, or a parrot." He looks up at the mule. "I'm a lone wolf."

Upon hearing this, Manuelito, eyes wide, brays moronically.

On the other side of the barn door Marlene smiles wisely and whispers to herself, "Uh-huh, a lone wolf. We'll see about that."

Moonlight sifts in through the cracks in the barn. The plants dry, hang quietly upside-down.

DAY THREE OF DRYING

Daren and Marlene remove the big sticky buds from the plants. They use scissors to manicure the buds, cutting off the single leaves.

"You think girls put a spell on guys they want?"

Marlene suspiciously lifts an eyebrow his way and continues working.

"No. Definitely not. Maybe."

HOUSE—LATER

Daren squeezes the long sticky buds in an improvised press. He cranks a handle. Pieces of wood move closer together, squashing the buds. This slow method doesn't appear to be working very well.

Marlene enters with a confident grin. "Hey, check this

out."

He follows her to the kitchen. She opens a cabinet to expose a trash compactor. "Who says Mexico is a third world country?"

LATER

Marlene and Daren weigh buds on a bathroom scale. They pack them into the trash compactor. Marlene presses the button; out pops a forty-pound rectangle of perfectly-pressed marijuana.

LATER

Marlene holds it open while Daren carefully lowers the bale into a burlap rice sack. Beside them, a big stack of bales in burlap sacks.

COUNTRYSIDE—NIGHT

Marlene drives the rickety mule wagon down a curvy mountain dirt road. The rifle in her lap points at Daren. The wagon goes over a bump and the rifle accidentally goes off: BANG! The bullet narrowly misses Daren's lap. "Hey! Watch that!"

The creaky wagon is stacked to the top with big burlap bales of the finest air-dried weed in all of Mexico. Manuelito, annoyed at having to pull the heavy wagon, brays loudly. They move precariously around a sharp turn that drops off a thousand feet on one side.

"Careful, Manuelito, this is the finest marijuana in all of Mexico."

One bale falls off the wagon. It rolls over the edge. And tumbles down the mountainside.

"Ooops, ho well, there goes about sixty thousand American dollars." Manuelito brays again.

"You're kidding. So what's all this stuff worth roughly anyway?"

"Oh, roughly, wholesale, about probably four American million dollars, give or take a few five hundred thousand."

"You're kidding me." He reaches over and turns the shotgun so it points out the wagon and not at him anymore.

"Nope."

Marlene still trying to calculate in her head. "No wait, maybe way more. Anyway Uncle Bictor would of wanted it this way. You and me partners, fifty-fifty." She spits on her hand, Daren spits on his and they shake hands. "Fifty-fifty".

ZIHUATENEJO HARBOR—SHORE—LATER

Marlene and Daren lift a bale off the wagon. She helps Daren load it into a heavy-duty black plastic garbage bag. They wrap duct tape around so the bales are totally waterproof and load them onto the surfboard. The mule brays loudly.

Daren floats four at a time on his surfboard and swims it out to *Outlaw*. Manuelito brays loudly again.

Marlene, "Shhhh Manuelito! Be very very quiet." The

mule brays again.

LATER

There are two bales left on the wagon. Daren paddles up on the surfboard. "That's all we can take."

"You sure?"

"I'm sure, we're full, actually over-full. Remember what your uncle said about not being greedy."

"Okay then."

She speaks into the mule's ear. "Manuelito, take the rest of this to the poor and to the orphans of the street." She smacks the mule's butt. Manuelito brays loudly and runs away like a lunatic, jerking the wagon toward the town.

OUTLAW—NIGHT

Marlene swims up to *Outlaw* and climbs onboard. Daren opens the hatch and removes the drop-boards. He shows Marlene that the entire boat is packed so tight with bales that they can't even go below. Marlene pulls folded aluminum-coated plastic tarps out of her bag, "Cover them up with these. So they won't show on infra-red imaging from the air." Daren pulls out several bales so he can crawl below on his stomach to spread the covering.

"You seem to know a lot about this."

"I'm Mexican, remember? We invented marijuana."

No running lights on, *Outlaw's* sails silently rise—and she sails sweetly out of the harbor into the night.

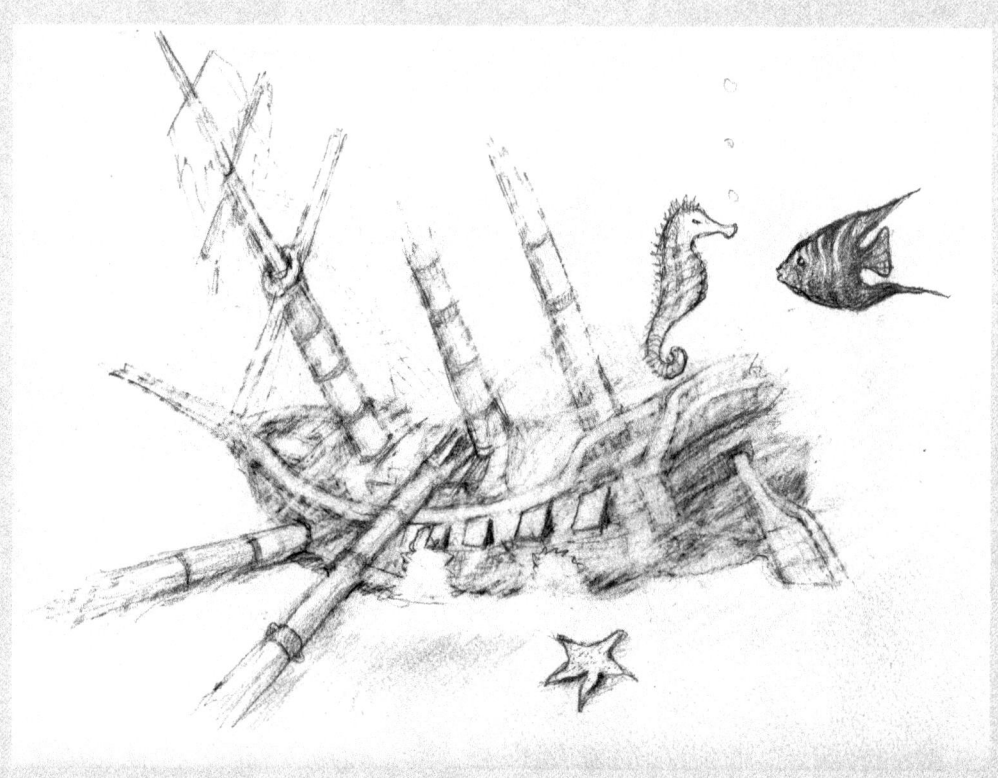

Pink Pearl Hunter

The pirate ship *Jackal's Head* sails on crystalline turquoise water—overhead, Man O'War Birds soar, but the mighty sea has other plans for *Jackal's Head*—a terrible storm is brewing, black clouds and waterspouts churn, wind saw-blades the ocean. Onboard the thrashing pirate ship the swarthy crew scramble to pull down sail while spray and angry waves hiss and break across the deck. Captain Black Jackal yells, "Hurry ye scarvy bilge worm. Brail the fore'course. Secure the main brace."

The storm is moving too fast. The pirate ship reels and heels as the wind and sea pound it with brutal angry fists. Sails rip, yardarms splinter and crash. The Helmsman struggles with the wheel. Black Jackal throws him aside. Grinding his rotten teeth, he tries hard to bring his ship up into the wind. He yells, "Harr there... lower the fore t'gallants". Too late; the foremast lets go and smashes to the deck.

Spray flying and wind howling. Over which we hear a loud grinding noise as Black Jackal's ship scrapes headlong over a jagged coral reef, tearing out its bottom.

And on this day, in squallish haze and driving rain, the dread pirate ship, *Jackal's Head,* will meet her cruel destiny, and havoc no more. She slowly slips below the surface and slides silently with all hands to her salty grave. We watch as the doomed ship *Jackal's Head* sinks—the gnarly crew hold onto rail and rigging, pinned and tangled in twisted spars, their feet trailing above them, they ride the ship down to the bottom of the stormy sea.

BEACH SHACK—SEBASTIAN ISLAND— CARIBBEAN—PRESENT DAY—BACKYARD

Where a rooster crows and chases a chicken, dust rising. A hermit crab peeks out of his shell. A papaya tree is pregnant with the promise of ripe, juicy fruit. Coconut palms curve and lean, their fronds whisper and dance to the soft tradewind.

Old Jake sits in a hand-made bamboo chair. By his dress and demeanor Jake appears to be a man both adventurous and worldly, relaxed and poised. He looks out past the surf at the sparkling jewel that spreads before him— the mythic Caribbean Ocean.

"Hi, name's Jake, yeah, glad to meet you too." He tips the front of his wide brim straw hat. "I am a Pink Pearl

Hunter, last of a dying breed, and this here is how my pink pearl hunting all began."

He leans the chair back picks up a stick and uses it to casually flick aside a medium-sized island boa constrictor. An old schooner at anchor lies offshore. He watches her roll for a moment in the gentle swell.

"I will tell you this to start—I was born into poverty in Homestead, Florida. When I was a boy of eight-years-old, my parents died and they sent me away to live here with my Uncle Jon. He had a sailboat. That one," he points his stick at a beautiful old wooden schooner.

UNCLE JON—50 YEARS BEFORE

The same beautiful wooden schooner, *Reef Chief,* sails gracefully on the bluest Caribbean—close to an island with white sand beaches and long leaning palms. The schooner turns into the wind and stops, her sails flutter. Only one man on deck, Uncle Jon. He lowers and ties up the sails. The anchor splashes over the bow, chain rattles on the bow roller and the anchor bites the sandy bottom. In the west, the evening sky is ablaze; a scud of dark clouds roll toward us, and thunder grumbles.

Later, Uncle Jon sits in a dim depressing drinking establishment on the Caribbean island of Sebastian. Thunder drums outside. Through the window and through sheets of rain we see his schooner *Reef Chief,* a tethered animal tugging on her anchor chain.

Outlaws

The bartender Limbo, a long lean rasta dreadlock with a pleasant smile, opens another bottle of beer for his only customer, Uncle Jon, an Irishman who lives by his wits and sleeps in his clothes, who drinks one of many beers this rainy night.

Uncle Jon mumbles, "Getting too old and tired for this crap anymore. What you think Limbo, should I sell my schooner an' move ashore?" Limbo wipes a dish with a dirty rag. "Lemme put it dis away, Jon. Right now, you da town drunk wit da schooner; you sell da boat, you be da town drunk."

The telephone rings. Limbo picks up, passes the receiver to Uncle Jon. "Fo' you." Uncle Jon takes it "Who'd call me here?" Limbo answers, "Where else could dey find you?"

"Yeah, what d'you want?" He raises one eyebrow "Yeah, he's my brother." His forehead wrinkles, "Dead? How? When?" He listens, "His son?" Suddenly sober, his eyes open wide, "No. No. No orphanage. Yeah, I'll take care of him. Put him on the morning flight to Sebastian." He listens to the voice on the other end. "Yes, I'm positive." He hangs up and finishes his beer.

Next day, Uncle Jon drinks a beer at a table; sitting with him, young Jake (a traumatized eight-year-old), looks at the menu. "Uncle, what's a conch fritter?" "Konk, 'tis pronounced konk. You'll be hearing that word around here a lot boy, food from the sea, food for the poor, food for the hungry. Limbo, bring this young man an order of your finest conch fritters if you please."

Raya, a perky eight-year-old island girl, walks up to Jake. Around her neck hangs a tiny conch shell on a string, "Hi, you d' new boy, my name's Raya, wanta be my friend, what your name?" Jake shyly looks down at his shoes, "Jake."

Rudy, a rough-looking burly local, lumbers up to the table. He pushes Raya away and glares down at Uncle Jon, "Where's me money?" Rudy pounds his huge fist twice on the table scaring young Jake. Uncle Jon pulls out some crumpled bills and pushes them into Rudy's hand. "Here. You'll get the rest next week. Now leave us."

Rudy counts the bills and stuffs them in his pocket, "How 'bout I jus' take da kid till you finish da pay-up?" Rudy lifts frightened Jake from his chair and carries him away squirming and kicking.

Uncle Jon swallows a quick gulp of beer. He puts down his bottle and wipes the foam off his mustache with the back of his hand. His eyes never leaving Big Rudy and Little Jake.

Rudy sets Jake down to open the door. Limbo looks at Uncle Jon and shakes his dread-lock head, "My, my, dat Rudy him mess wit da wrong man." Uncle Jon: "Watch my beer Limbo."

Uncle Jon plasters Big Rudy into the wall with a flying

tackle and rides him down to the floor. Rudy kicks and punches. Uncle Jon places only his thumb on a pressure point under Rudy's jaw that temporarily paralyzes him, making his whole body go limp. Jake looks down at them wide-eyed. "Don't ever touch my kid again. You got that? You'll get your money."

Uncle Jon and young Jake sit back down at the table. Rudy lies on the ground, eyes glazed, his whole body twitching like he's just been electrocuted. Limbo brings Uncle Jon a fresh beer, helps Rudy find his feet and aims him out the door. Uncle Jon leans in and says softly to Jake, "Eat your fritters... son." Across the room, Raya smiles sweetly at Jake.

Out the window, Schooner *Reef Chief* dances on the waves. Nearby a whale spouts, dives and shows her tail.

Next day, Jake stares blankly at the water.

Uncle Jon: "What's up?"

Jake: "I'm bored. There's nothing to do here, we don't even have a television."

"Oh yeah? Bored are you? Only one good cure for boredom." In one slick motion, Uncle Jon scoops Jake up and tosses him into the ocean. Jake flaps and splashes around in his wet clothes. When he calms down and looks up, his uncle says, "Wake up, open your eyes, son. Look around at this beautiful world. The waves, the birds, the ocean, the clouds, the trees, the starry sky. The world and its infinite intricacies is yours to discover."

Next day sailing, Uncle Jon gives Jake the wheel -"Supposed to be the wreck of an old pirate ship round here somewheres, with a huge conch pearl—the rarest, most expensive gem in the world."

"Do you know where it is?"

"Oh I've looked for it. Just about everyone has. But nobody's ever found it."

Uncle Jon points to the fore sail, "Now watch." He eases the fore sheet. "See how the sail ripples and flutters right behind the mast like a wet cat?"

Jake nods, "Yeah."

"It's luffing. Sheet 'er in till the point when it just stops luffing. Like this." He sheets the sail in until it forms a smooth foil, the sailboat speeds up. "There, the sweet spot where the sail has the most power." He eases the sail until it luffs again and sheets it in. Now you try it."

Ashore at Uncle Jon's beach shack, Uncle Jon is passed out in his chair at a small table. His big hand still curled around the bottle of rum which he can't seem to let go of even in his sleep. Little Jake respectfully lifts his uncle's big head and slides a soft pillow under it.

Uncle Jon stands beside Jake (now an enthusiastic ten-year-old) on deck of the schooner beneath the stars.

"That bright one there, see it?" Jake follows Uncle Jon's finger as he points to a star.

"Yes."

"Brightest star in the sky. Sirius."

"Yeah, neat."

"And that bright planet, Venus, the closest planet to Earth, it turns so fast around the sun and spins so slow, that a day is longer than a year. The temperature is over 900 degrees, and when it rains, it rains sulphuric acid. There have been a few space landings, the longest one lasted two minutes before it melted."

While Jake looks up at the other stars, Uncle Jon pulls a bottle of rum from his pocket and twists off the cap.

Jake asks, "Why do you always drink that stuff?"

"And that is a very good question, son. I used to drink because I was lonely..." Uncle Jon looks at the rum and down at little Jake and throws the bottle at the starry sky. "But now, with you, son, I'm not lonely anymore."

⌣⌐

"That said, Uncle Jon never drank a drop of alcohol again and became my true father."

⌣⌐

Jake smiles, points at another star, "What's that one?"

⌣⌐

Jake, a confident fourteen-year-old, braces himself against the dive ladder holding a sextant, his eye tracking the sun. Jake: "Mark." Uncle Jon clicks a chronometer.

Jake: "Mark. Fourteen degrees, thirty-six minutes, twenty-five seconds."

"You sure about the thirty-six minutes?"

Jake looks at the brass sextant arc again: "Sorry, thirty-four minutes."

"Don't be sorry my boy. Every minute off on that sextant of yours, you're a mile off on your navigation."

"Won't happen again."

An Osprey appears. Jake whistles the call of an Osprey; the Osprey answers his call.

"See them clouds there?" Uncle Jon points to a long string of clouds with dark spots in them. "Turtle track clouds, they appear only when the sea turtle climbs up the beach to lay her eggs." Jake looks up at the cloud. Jake grabs hold of the handrail as he moves forward along the wet deck. Uncle Jon adds, "A sound head, an honest heart, and a humble spirit are the three best guides through time and eternity." He grabs his heart, makes a fist and grimaces in pain, whispering "Good work son. Good work. Good boy."

⟵⟶

"Uncle Jon lost all his tools and equipment in hurricane

Ivan and we fell on hard times."

⁓

Jake, sixteen years old, strong and sweating, uses a machete to chop down sugar cane. Beside him, Uncle Jon and a few others, down-on-their-luck; Jake and Uncle Jon, the only whites. These are poor and desperate men to be working so hard in the blazing afternoon Caribbean sun.

Uncle Jon pokes his machete into the earth. He wipes his brow. He holds a glass jug of water to his cracked lips and takes a sip. He passes the jug to the old dark-skinned man beside him who stops, lifts the jug to his dry lips and drinks. Uncle Jon pulls off his shirt, rips the sleeve off, and wraps it around the dark-skinned man's cut hand. "Bless you brother Jon. Bless you." They continue chopping cane.

⁓

"And finding work where we could. I don't know, it was like there was some kind of curse on Uncle Jon. Every business scheme ended in disaster. I hated being poor and vowed that someday I would break the curse and we'd be rich."

⁓

A mean-looking plantation boss man drives a beat-up old Jeep along a dirt cane-field road, dust funnels behind and rises above the tall sugar cane. He wears a blue shirt with stripes on his sleeve. As he drives by rows and rows of sugar cane, he sees a monkey. He skids the Jeep to a stop, backs up, pulls out a rifle, aims and shoots.

Jake, alone, chops down a stand of sugar cane. Something catches his eye. He parts the thick cane. A dead spider monkey lies in the dry earth, a red bullet-hole in her back. Jake hears a squeaking sound and sinks to his knees. Flies buzz. Hiding underneath its mother, a tiny female spider monkey looks up at him. He drops the machete and reaches out to gently touch her. The baby Monkey grabs onto Jake's finger with both little black hands. The Monkey makes a sound to Jake. Jake replicates the sound. He picks her up. "I can never replace your mother, little monkey." He remembers sitting scared in the bar first time he met Uncle Jon—"But I can be your uncle, and I won't ever let anyone hurt you again." He puts the little Monkey into his backpack and continues chopping cane. Her little dark eyes peek out.

Jake holds his backpack up to Raya, now a pretty tropical island flower of sixteen. He pulls it open. Raya melts at the sight of the baby Monkey, "Oh Jake, she so sweet." Jake asks her, "How d'you say monkey in Spanish?"

"El mono."

"We'll call her Monolita."

Outlaws

Schooner *Reef Chief* sails gracefully, Man O' War birds overhead. Jake at the wheel, tears in his eyes.

After he died, his closest friends gathered to pay their respect and to set Uncle Jon's ashes out to sea. His friends stand silent at the lee rail wearing brightly colored clothes.

Limbo, Rudy, the old Black Men who chopped cane beside them, Raya, and others we've seen on the island—a tear in each eye. They take turns to shake out Uncle Jon's dead ashes from inside a pink Queen Conch shell. One dark-skinned island woman spreads a handful of ash. Her long fingers carefully pass the shell on to the next person, then she kisses her dusty fingertips and points them at the ocean.

They spread his dead ash onto a welcoming tropical ocean writhing with life.

Dolphins swim alongside, weaving back and forth in his ash as if collecting Uncle Jon and taking him away to a sacred place, flying fish leap from the inky blue surface, they fly through the air, tilting in a graceful arc of silvery wings before they disappear.

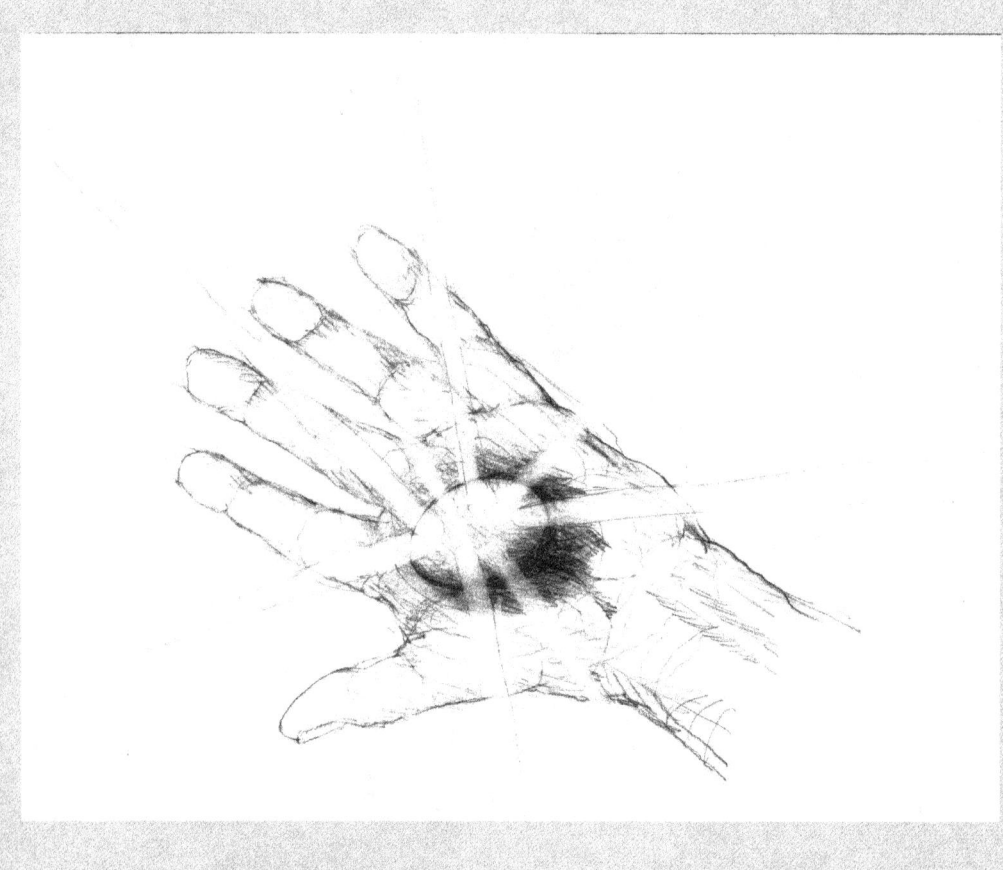

Pink Pearl Hunter, Part Two

"After he died I inherited Uncle Jon's beach shack and schooner and started an inter-island trading business. I went into the cargo delivery business. But I inherited his bad business luck too."

While Jake raises sails, behind his back, his pet monkey, Monolita, now full grown, throws a fire extinguisher overboard, puts her hand over her mouth and giggles.

Schooner *Reef Chief* swings to her anchor as Jake rows cargo ashore in the old rowboat loaded with crates of rum. Behind his back Monolita pulls a bottle of rum from a crate. She looks at it, smiles and quietly drops it into the ocean and another and another.

Back on the schooner underway, Monolita chatters to herself as she swings from the boom. Jake at the wheel

179

steering. Bubbly waves softly press against her hull as the schooner slices through the sea. When Jake isn't looking, Monolita sneaks up, drops his binoculars overboard and giggles.

A big dark storm approaches fast. Black clouds. Water-spouts. Air white with rain. Wind gusts scratch out waves on the obsidian-turquoise surface of the sea—jagged they rise, marching in rows like angry white horses, raging towards Jake's schooner, which suddenly appears fragile and vulnerable.

Jake pulls down the foresail. The mainsail jibes over with a crash. Jake heaves down that sail too. Monolita jumps up and down, spins the wheel in both directions and holds her hands over her eyes. The schooner is out of control. Jake secures the sails. He races back to take the wheel. He stares ahead through white mist and stinging rain. Monolita hugs his leg. *Reef Chief,* still sailing hard under jib alone, wildly charges ahead.

Monolita, scared, jumps into Jake's arms. *Reef Chief* rocking, rolling on the waves. An improperly secured anchor bumps off the fore deck and crashes overboard into the ocean. Anchor chain rattles over the bow. Coming to an abrupt stop at the end of the chain, *Reef Chief* swings around as her anchor digs its teeth into the bottom of the sea. Monolita hides in Jake's arms, puts her hands over Jake's ears and shrieks frantically.

Next morning, storm over, *Reef Chief* swings calmly at

her anchor. Jake awakes at the wheel, startling himself by his loud snoring. He rubs his eyes at the rising sun. Monolita wakes too. She hangs on Jake with her arms around his shoulders like a hairy backpack. Jake stands up and looks below. Monolita peeks over Jake's shoulder at the overturned cases of rum and all the broken bottles. Jake sits on the cabin top with his head in his hands. "I'm ruined." He sighs. Monolita points an imaginary gun at her head. She pulls the imaginary trigger and lies down on the deck with her tongue hanging out, playing dead.

Jake tries to raise the anchor, but it's really stuck. The straining anchor winch smokes. Jake pulls off his shirt. Monolita imitates him. Jake puts on his mask and snorkel. He slides into his dive fins. He jumps into the clear blue ocean and turns to Monolita, "Now behave Monolita!" The Monkey, wearing an upside-down dive mask, looks over the side—where did Uncle Jake go?

She makes concerned monkey noises. Jake swims down the anchor chain. He almost reaches the bottom but surfaces to gasp a noisy lung full of air. He dives in again, swimming faster. When he reaches the bottom—he can't believe his eyes. His anchor is fouled in the ancient wreck of a big old wooden ship.

Jake swims back to his schooner and rushes up the ladder. Onboard he straps on a scuba tank and weight belt. He grabs his underwater flashlight, jumps in again, kicks back down along the anchor chain until he reaches the bottom.

He swims around examining what is left of the ancient wreck, brushes a clump of seaweed off the transom revealing the words *"Jackal's Head"* and crudely carved below, a Skull and Bones. His eyes are wide behind the dive mask. He swims around the spooky old hulk and wriggles through the broken timbers.

Jake enters the wreck, turns on his underwater flashlight and looks around. He pushes open the creaky door to the Captain's Quarters.

Something black sticks up through the sand in the corner of the tilting cabin. He digs around feeling something. He stops. Stirred-up silt blurs the room.

As it slowly clears, he sees a small treasure chest and a rusty sword. With a scraping and a ringing sound, he pries open the lid with the sword. Inside another smaller box. Inside that one, the largest Pink Conch Pearl he'd ever seen. Jake remembers Uncle Jon saying, *"pink conch pearls are the rarest, most valuable gems in the world."*

He shines his flashlight on this huge pink radiating gem. He reaches out for it, hears a rumbling sound and freezes. He aims his flashlight as a huge black Marine Iguana the size of a large crocodile sticks his ugly massive head through the creaking door and bares its teeth.

"Now I've seen a lot of weird anomalies in my travels, but

I must admit, I have never seen a carnivorous electric marine iguana as monstrous and mean-looking as this one."

Its mouth opens exposing double rows of razor-jagged teeth. It slowly slithers into the cabin glaring intently at Jake, big enough around to swallow him whole. More and more of it enters until the monster fills the entire cabin, its beady eyes watch him, blue barbs of lightning crackle from its nostrils. The iguana lunges and snaps at Jake. Jake ducks out of the way. Jake snatches the giant pink pearl. He slides it into the pocket of his weight belt and swims out of the cabin fast, slamming the door on the monstrous carnivore.

Breathing hard, kicking fast, he swims up to his fouled anchor and untangles it from the wreckage. Meanwhile the angry Marine Iguana punches through the side of the ship with its head. Bam! Bam! Bam! Jake looks around nervously and swims up to the surface slower than his slowest bubbles to be on the safe side. The huge, lumbering Marine Iguana follows; blue electric lightning bolts snap from its nostrils.

Monolita jumps up and down, screeches and holds her hands over her eyes, peeking out through her fingers as Jake swims fast with the giant Marine Iguana in close pursuit. Jake grabs the ladder. He tosses his flippers up on deck he snatches a quick glance back over his shoulder at the approaching angry monster. When Jake climbs back on board Monolita hugs him. He removes his weight belt and scuba tank. The boat shudders as the Marine Iguana punches into it with his head. Monolita screeches loudly.

Jake grabs his sextant, takes a quick sun shot, and consults his watch. He writes down numbers, and marks an "X" on the chart. Jake looks up to the blue sky, "I found your Pirate Ship, Uncle Jon. Do you hear me? I found your Pirate ship!"

The monster sea reptile pounds into the schooner again. BAM! Jake heaves up the chain and anchor. Then he hoists the sails.

While Jake is busy, Monolita opens the pocket of Jake's weight belt. She pulls out the huge pink conch pearl, holds it in both black hands, looks at it, smiles and drops it into the vast blue ocean.

"I spent the rest of my life searching for that huge conch pearl."

Lucky

Desperately cold, I shiver down a dark, empty, grey street in some frozen heart-dead Nebraska town—Lungs ache; nostrils, eyelashes frozen; fingers, toes numb. I just want to lie down. Will I be the fifteen-year-old runaway they find frozen to death, curled up in a deserted alley? No, no, I have to, have to keep moving, keep walking, keep moving, or die.

An American Indian girl, one green eye, one brown, steps out in front of me, stops me with her body—*no no have to keep moving have to keep moving.*

"Hi, I'm Lucky." She flicks her head, long shiny black horse-tail hair floats to one side. "God if you don't got the bluest angel eyes I ever seen. Where you live, boy?"

"No place…I live…no… place."

"Where's your family? Yer kin at?"

"Got no."

She halfway unzips her silver-studded black leather jacket and leans in to me, letting it open so I can see her bare skin inside—*how is it she is not frozen, like me?*

She reaches into her pocket and pulls out a stick of gum, unwraps it and presses it past my shivering teeth into my mouth, whispering, "Let's go up t' the Lincoln Hotel an' fuck until we catch fire."

"Catch fire...catch fire...did...did she say...catch fire?"

It didn't matter that she was probably waiting for the next guy, any guy, to walk down that street. It didn't matter that we were strangers. Another day, another girl, it might have mattered, but that night, that night it didn't matter, that night it didn't matter at all.

We walk—every frozen breath torches my lungs—we turn the corner—bumping hips we walk—shivering— steaming breath we walk.

"You don't talk much, I like that."

The front door of the Lincoln Hotel is boarded up; she pries it open. We duck inside, out of the ragged, knife-edge of ice-sharp wind.

She climbs the dark rickety narrow steps—in front of me—I am close, close, close to her heat—I taste her warm curves somewhere deep inside my frozen tongue. Her heat pulls me—closer, closer, closer to her—my heart bumps hard—racing—pounding—my heart lifting up out of my shivering chest—we climb up, up, up to room number 408.

She presses the glowing furnace of her body into mine against the door. The heat of her warm tongue in my mouth tastes of blues songs—smoky rooms—broken hearts—tears—warm cheap whiskey—and sad stale cigarettes. Blood thunders my head.

The door creaks open like a graveyard gate. We stumble into the room. The window frozen open. Yellow-stained dusty lace curtains dance on crystal waves of frozen wind into the cold ghost-dark hotel room.

She unbuttons my Levis. I unzip her tight torn black jeans and hold the sweet weight of her warm breasts, smooth with intoxicating girl-skin-oil. She kicks, her pants slide across the floor.

We pile tent blankets over our bodies on the bed. I kneel to pull my bulky jacket and sweatshirt over my head—her dark eyes glint—my shivering muscles claw at my ribcage—greedy for her heat again.

Lucky—an arcane she-animal—moves slow and softly over me—warm black crow-feather hair paints my icy skin—she breathes hot breaths on me—the heat from her melts my frozen skin—we roll together over and over and over…

I wake up. Alone. Cold. Naked. I pull on my pants, button them, shivering again, and when I look for the rest of my clothes—my boots—my wallet—all gone—everything gone—and—a note written in black lipstick on the window:

Forever – Lucky

A night security guard lends me some clothes and boots and hooks me up over at the factory. I work for a week, load 90-pound bags of cement onto boxcars. With my first paycheck, I buy me some new boots and a warm jacket.

At night I search the streets for her. I sit on the steps of the boarded-up Lincoln Hotel, and not with anger, but because my body aches for her. I ask around. But nobody'd ever heard of an Indian girl called Lucky.

But the wail of the freight trains pulls at the scattered strings of my wandering soul and when I can't fight off the curse no more, I give up looking for her and jump a boxcar rolling south and another rolling west into California.

I can't get Lucky off my mind. The clattering iron wheels and the train whistle call her name. When I closed my eyes—I see her eyes—every cigarette reminds me of the taste of her—every match, the heat inside of her.

Lucky

A week later, I meet up with Cochise, an old, one-armed Comanche Indian in a boxcar outside of Fresno. I ask if he knew her, a girl called Lucky. He stops for a time and then he tells me:

"Yes… I once knew a beautiful young Lakota runaway girl from Wamblee, South Dakota… she called herself Lucky… she had one green eye and one brown eye… oh… but… that one… that one… they found curled up in an alley… froze to death… one unusually cold winter night… near some thirty years ago… in Lincoln Nebraska."

Passage to Montedenero

We was rolling south b'southwest from Valpraiso to Montedenero on the wretched tops'l schooner, *Goodwind*, with a cargo o' general perishable.

We run into a number o' storms, was beset by crazy pirates, revenue cutters, an' large foul-smellin' sea monkeys on that passage.

The Capt'n died two days out o' syphilis an' his first mate Shidbran, (we called him Shitbrain), went an' got us lost off of New Garponset in fog s' thick you could reach out an' light a match on it.

Fog cleared to half gale so we ran under reefed fores'l an' storm jib fer three days up past Langoon's Head Light. On the fourth day, number three hatch let go, an' carried away overboard an' our cargo did got loose. T'was too rough t' secure so we just had to re-sign to let it all bash 'round till the seas calm'd down some.

Then Shitbrain got into the rum keg an' locked hisself in the sail locker so the ships' carpenter, Chips took the wheel an' set us on a broad reach for Montedenero.

We off'd the mains'l an' ran b'fore a full gale soon after roundin' Langoon's Head an' musta took green water on deck fer five straight days 'n a row. Then the fores'l carried away when the fore preventer let go an' knocked Stew, the cook, overboard.

We couldn't a go back fer him fer fear a bein' broached on them big bastard mountains o' snarlin' seas, so we threwd him a life preserver an' a can o cookies an' sailed onward, never 'xpectin' to see Stew agin, an' not bein' able to jibe 'round fer him we all wish'd him peace, sweet dreams, an' everlastin' tran-quill-ity.

Middle o' that night we hard this loud THUMP-THUMP on deck an' when we lit the starboard deck lantern, we sees alayin' there—a frickin' nakid MER-MAID!

She was a green an' scaley beauty an' 'ad long blonde hair fulla seaweed an' sliberin' sea horses. She flapped an' flipped on deck tryin' to get her green self ov'r the bul-warks back inta th' frothy brine.

None o' us never havin' seed no mer-maid b'fore, watch'd 'er flip an' flap in tha moon-light. Coupla deckhands went t' help 'er back over the caprail but soon's they touch'd 'er, they was turn'd inta mackerel an' flipped an' flapped beside 'er on the deck till they done jump'd ov'rboard an' swarm away.

Just 'bout then, the stormjib blew an' kick'd so hard that we hadta haul it down afore it broke'd the head-stay. When we come back t' where that there Mer-maid was a layin'—damnit if she weren't gone!

Next day the storm blew'd itself out an' we sew'd the fores'l, an' raised the mains'l, fores'l, fisherman stays'l, an' yankee jib, an' put 'er on a beam reach fer Montedenero agin. The storm had blow'd us 'bout two hundred sev-en-ty miles south but now we was once agin sweet beam reachin' for our des-tin-ation.

All hands eagerly collected cargo an' it was carfully stack'd back down b'low in number 3. We was repairin' tore sails an' broke riggin' an' runnin' new prevent'rs when Tooth-less Jack noticed somethin' astickin' out from under the liferaft tarp. He pull'd back the tarp t'find the Mer-maid, soundly asleep-ing.

Careful not t' touch her an' suffer bein' turned inta mack-erels, we all gather'd round t' oggle at 'er fine an' shapely bo-dy. She were damn pretty'r 'n any skank woman none of us never see'd on land, thar weren't a man aboard who din't e-magine havin' sweet inter-course with that fishy beau-ty where she lay, but none dared touch 'er for fear o' bein' turned inta slimy fishes.

I covered her up an' she slept like that fer six days an' six nights, an' ol' Charlie Rimsworth took it upon hisself t' keep 'er hosed down regular so's she wouldn't dry up none too much. One night we hard some flappin' an' flippin on deck. T'was poor Rimsworth, couldn't resist temp-ta-tion an' was turn'd inta a hall-i-but, a flippin' an' a flappin' for the salty open sea.

I cover'd her nakid body with the storm jib. "I get scared at night" she said to me. So I slept on deck b'side 'er an' told 'er I was sorry fer the behavior of me mates and that I would never hurt 'er an' would alweys protect 'er from thems that would.

When the sun come up one morn, seven weeks outa Valparaiso, there were Mount Montedenero hove off th' starb'rd bow! We haul'd tha diamon' fluke rock pick up on deck, shackled the sonofabitch t' stud-link anchor chain an' lower'd it threw the starb'rd hawse pipe.

We jibed 'round Pukers Point an' handed tha yankee, mains'l, fores'l, fish'rman stays'l, an' mains'l. We let go the anchor in Plasmar Cove an' whilst the anchor chain rat-tled over the capstan wildcat an' the anchor bit its teeth inta the rocky bottom, the Mer-maid stood up on 'er tail, blew'd me a big fat kiss, an' jumped over the taff rail, an' swarm away.

Well, y' might see me one day at a waterfront pub or ta-kin' a piss offa th' seawall an' think he's jus' a crazy ol' fool with a goofy smile on 'is face.

Oh, but e-ver-y night when I comes home to me little

sailboat an' goes to sleep, thar hasn't been a night since that fateful passage from Valparaiso to Montedenero, that me secret best friend, that thar beau-ti-ful fishy green Mer-maid weren't sweetly waitin' in me bunk fo' me an' I tells 'er every night as I untangle green sea horses from 'er hair, that I would never hurt 'er an' would alweys protect 'er from thems that would.

Outlaw

Suzi whispers that she loves me
As she lies beside me on the bed
She kissed me hard and cried my name
You have to leave she said.

Her bedroom door burst open
A gunman in the way
Was Sheriff Spade, mean and angry
She was his fiancée.

I grabbed my pants and charged him
The first shot missed my snout
His pistol hot, it fired a shot
And blew his knee cap out.

In a burst of glass I jumped out
Through the window to the street
I ran through hill and mountain
Through canyon and sand beach.

Outlaws

For every case he couldn't solve
Spade blamed the crime on me.
For a beer, a smoke, or a bottle of wine
A witness swore t'was I he did see.

They blamed me for a murder
A fire and a brawl
A rape, a knife, a shooting
I'm running from the law.

They hunted me with hound dog
With plane and car and gun
I'm always two steps ahead of them
I'm always on the run.

Jumped the fence at Walla Walla
Swam away from Alcatraz
Every post office has my picture
Every sheriff wants my ass.

Bounty men they are a-coming
Train-yard bulls are creepin' close
If they catch me tonight they'll fry me good
They'll burn my skin to toast.

Every schoolgirl writes me love letters
Every farmer knows my name
If the lawmen ever catch me
They'll hang me just the same.

My daddy was an outlaw
My ma a prostitute

My gramma robbed the city bank
And gambled away the loot.

They hanged my baby brother
They cooked my sister Ned
If they catch my skinny butt tonight
I too will wind up dead.

The politicians hate me
I've exposed their evil ways
For that I am an outlaw
They'll hunt me to my grave.

My best friend's my six shooter,
A car, a horse, a train
The poster says I'm dangerous
They all say I'm insane.

Pretty women screw my body
Cruel jailers screw my mind
The only home I ever know'd was
Moving down the line.

Won't live to be a hundred
No rocking chair for me
A piney box, a shallow grave
Five feet down I'll be.

The moon and stars my buddies
The silver rail's my pal
If I get to live another day
It will be a miracle.

Outlaws

I have no place to run to
I have no place to hide
I have no friend, no pretty girl
To call my name and cry.

But now I'm tired a-runnin'
Like a rabbit from the law
I'll stand my ground and fight the fight
Like a tired and proud outlaw.

The wind can have my pistols
The stars my spurs and hat
The moon my buckskin saddle
The campfire my lariat.

I ask nothing from the Eagle
I ask nothing from the Sea
I ask nothing from the Mountain Lake
But that they all remember me.